"I have never read anything quite like Mark Haddon's funny and agonizingly honest book, or encountered a narrator more vivid and memorable. I advise you to buy two copies; you won't want to lend yours out."
—Arthur Golden, author of *Memoirs of a Geisha*

"At once funny and achingly sad, this thought-provoking debut may leave us wondering if our worn coping skills are really any better than Christopher's."
—*The News & Observer*

"Filled with humor and pain, [*The Curious Incident of the Dog in the Night-Time*] verges on profundity."
—*San Jose Mercury News*

"*The Curious Incident of the Dog in the Night-Time* brims with imagination, empathy, and vision—plus it's a lot of fun to read." —Myla Goldberg, author of *Bee Season*

MARK   HADDON

THE   CURIOUS   INCIDENT
OF   THE   DOG   IN   THE   NIGHT-TIME

Mark Haddon is a writer and illustrator of numerous
award-winning children's books and television screen-
plays. As a young man, Haddon worked with autistic
individuals. He teaches creative writing for the Arvon
Foundation and lives in Oxford, England.

THE CURIOUS INCIDENT

OF THE DOG IN THE NIGHT-TIME

. . . .

MARK HADDON

Vintage Contemporaries

Vintage Books   A Division of Random House, Inc.   New York

THE

CURIOUS INCIDENT

. . . .

OF THE DOG

. . . .

IN THE NIGHT-TIME

. . . .

FIRST VINTAGE CONTEMPORARIES OPEN-MARKET EDITION, APRIL 2004

The Library or Congress has cataloged the Doubleday edition as follows:
Haddon, Mark.
The curious incident of the dog in the night-time : a novel / Mark Haddon—1st ed.
p. cm.
Despite his overwhelming fear of interacting with people, Christopher, a mathematically gifted, autistic fifteen-year-old boy, decides to investigate the murder of a neighbor's dog and uncovers secret information about his mother.
[1. Autism—Fiction. 2. Savants (Savant syndrome)—Fiction. 3. England—Fiction.]
I. Title
PZ7.H1165 Cu 2003
[Fic]—dc21   2002031355

Vintage Open-Market ISBN: 1-4000-7783-4

Book design by Maria Carella

www.vintagebooks.com

Manufactured in the United States of America
50 49 48 47 46

This book
is dedicated to
Sos

. . . . . .

With thanks to
Kathryn Heyman, Clare Alexander,
Kate Shaw and Dave Cohen

THE CURIOUS INCIDENT
OF THE DOG IN THE NIGHT-TIME

. . . .

2.   It was 7 minutes after midnight. The dog was lying on the grass in the middle of the lawn in front of Mrs. Shears's house. Its eyes were closed. It looked as if it was running on its side, the way dogs run when they think they are chasing a cat in a dream. But the dog was not running or asleep. The dog was dead. There was a garden fork sticking out of the dog. The points of the fork must have gone all the way through the dog and into the ground because the fork had not fallen over. I decided that the dog was probably killed with the fork because I could not see any other wounds in the dog and I do not think you would stick a garden fork into a dog after it had died for some other reason, like cancer, for example, or a road accident. But I could not be certain about this.

I went through Mrs. Shears's gate, closing it behind me. I walked onto her lawn and knelt beside the dog. I put my hand on the muzzle of the dog. It was still warm.

The dog was called Wellington. It belonged to Mrs. Shears,

who was our friend. She lived on the opposite side of the road, two houses to the left.

Wellington was a poodle. Not one of the small poodles that have hairstyles but a big poodle. It had curly black fur, but when you got close you could see that the skin underneath the fur was a very pale yellow, like chicken.

I stroked Wellington and wondered who had killed him, and why.

3. My name is Christopher John Francis Boone. I know all the countries of the world and their capital cities and every prime number up to 7,057.

Eight years ago, when I first met Siobhan, she showed me this picture

and I knew that it meant "sad," which is what I felt when I found the dead dog.

Then she showed me this picture

and I knew that it meant "happy," like when I'm reading about the Apollo space missions, or when I am still awake at 3 a.m. or 4 a.m. in the morning and I can walk up and down the street and pretend that I am the only person in the whole world.

Then she drew some other pictures

but I was unable to say what these meant.

I got Siobhan to draw lots of these faces and then write down next to them exactly what they meant. I kept the piece of paper in my pocket and took it out when I didn't understand what someone was saying. But it was very difficult to decide which of the diagrams was most like the face they were making because people's faces move very quickly.

When I told Siobhan that I was doing this, she got out a pencil and another piece of paper and said it probably made people feel very

and then she laughed. So I tore the original piece of paper up and threw it away. And Siobhan apologized. And now if I don't know what someone is saying, I ask them what they mean or I walk away.

5. I pulled the fork out of the dog and lifted him into my arms and hugged him. He was leaking blood from the fork holes.

I like dogs. You always know what a dog is thinking. It has

four moods. Happy, sad, cross and concentrating. Also, dogs are faithful and they do not tell lies because they cannot talk.

I had been hugging the dog for 4 minutes when I heard screaming. I looked up and saw Mrs. Shears running toward me from the patio. She was wearing pajamas and a housecoat. Her toenails were painted bright pink and she had no shoes on.

She was shouting, "What in fuck's name have you done to my dog?"

I do not like people shouting at me. It makes me scared that they are going to hit me or touch me and I do not know what is going to happen.

"Let go of the dog," she shouted. "Let go of the fucking dog for Christ's sake."

I put the dog down on the lawn and moved back 2 meters.

She bent down. I thought she was going to pick the dog up herself, but she didn't. Perhaps she noticed how much blood there was and didn't want to get dirty. Instead she started screaming again.

I put my hands over my ears and closed my eyes and rolled forward till I was hunched up with my forehead pressed onto the grass. The grass was wet and cold. It was nice.

7.   This is a murder mystery novel.

Siobhan said that I should write something I would want to read myself. Mostly I read books about science and maths. I do not like proper novels. In proper novels people say things like, "I am veined with iron, with silver and with streaks of common mud. I cannot contract into the firm fist which those clench who do not depend on stimulus."[1] What does this mean? I do not know. Nor does Father. Nor does Siobhan or Mr. Jeavons. I have asked them.

Siobhan has long blond hair and wears glasses which are made of green plastic. And Mr. Jeavons smells of soap and wears brown shoes that have approximately 60 tiny circular holes in each of them.

But I do like murder mystery novels. So I am writing a murder mystery novel.

In a murder mystery novel someone has to work out who the murderer is and then catch them. It is a puzzle. If it is a good puzzle you can sometimes work out the answer before the end of the book.

Siobhan said that the book should begin with something to grab people's attention. That is why I started with the dog. I also started with the dog because it happened to me and I find it hard to imagine things which did not happen to me.

Siobhan read the first page and said that it was different. She put this word into inverted commas by making the wiggly quotation sign with her first and second fingers. She said that it was usually people who were killed in murder mystery novels. I said that two dogs were killed in **The Hound of the Baskervilles,** the hound itself and James Mortimer's spaniel, but Siobhan said they weren't the victims of the murder, Sir Charles Baskerville was. She said that this was because readers cared more about people than dogs, so if a person was killed in a book, readers would want to carry on reading.

[1] I found this in a book when Mother took me into the library in town in 1996.

I said that I wanted to write about something real and I knew people who had died but I did not know any people who had been killed, except Mr. Paulson, Edward's father from school, and that was a gliding accident, not murder, and I didn't really know him. I also said that I cared about dogs because they were faithful and honest, and some dogs were cleverer and more interesting than some people. Steve, for example, who comes to the school on Thursdays, needs help to eat his food and could not even fetch a stick. Siobhan asked me not to say this to Steve's mother.

11. Then the police arrived. I like the police. They have uniforms and numbers and you know what they are meant to be doing. There was a policewoman and a policeman. The policewoman had a little hole in her tights on her left ankle and a red scratch in the middle of the hole. The policeman had a big orange leaf stuck to the bottom of his shoe which was poking out from one side.

The policewoman put her arms round Mrs. Shears and led her back toward the house.

I lifted my head off the grass.

The policeman squatted down beside me and said, "Would you like to tell me what's going on here, young man?"

I sat up and said, "The dog is dead."

"I'd got that far," he said.

I said, "I think someone killed the dog."

"How old are you?" he asked.

I replied, "I am 15 years and 3 months and 2 days."

"And what, precisely, were you doing in the garden?" he asked.

"I was holding the dog," I replied.

"And why were you holding the dog?" he asked.

This was a difficult question. It was something I wanted to do. I like dogs. It made me sad to see that the dog was dead.

I like policemen, too, and I wanted to answer the question properly, but the policeman did not give me enough time to work out the correct answer.

"Why were you holding the dog?" he asked again.

"I like dogs," I said.

"Did you kill the dog?" he asked.

I said, "I did not kill the dog."

"Is this your fork?" he asked.

I said, "No."

"You seem very upset about this," he said.

He was asking too many questions and he was asking them too quickly. They were stacking up in my head like loaves in the factory where Uncle Terry works. The factory is a bakery and he operates the slicing machines. And sometimes a slicer is not working fast enough but the bread keeps coming and there is a blockage. I sometimes think of my mind as a machine, but not always as a bread-slicing machine. It makes it easier to explain to other people what is going on inside it.

The policeman said, "I am going to ask you once again . . ."

I rolled back onto the lawn and pressed my forehead to the ground again and made the noise that Father calls groaning. I make this noise when there is too much information coming into my head from the outside world. It is like when you are upset and you hold the radio against your ear and you tune it halfway

7

between two stations so that all you get is white noise and then you turn the volume right up so that this is all you can hear and then you know you are safe because you cannot hear anything else.

The policeman took hold of my arm and lifted me onto my feet.

I didn't like him touching me like this.

And this is when I hit him.

13. This will not be a funny book. I cannot tell jokes because I do not understand them. Here is a joke, as an example. It is one of Father's.

His face was drawn but the curtains were real.

I know why this is meant to be funny. I asked. It is because *drawn* has three meanings, and they are **(1)** drawn with a pencil, **(2)** exhausted, and **(3)** pulled across a window, and meaning **1** refers to both the face and the curtains, meaning **2** refers only to the face, and meaning **3** refers only to the curtains.

If I try to say the joke to myself, making the word mean the three different things at the same time, it is like hearing three different pieces of music at the same time, which is uncomfortable and confusing and not nice like white noise. It is like three people trying to talk to you at the same time about different things.

And that is why there are no jokes in this book.

17. The policeman looked at me for a while without speaking. Then he said, "I am arresting you for assaulting a police officer."

This made me feel a lot calmer because it is what policemen say on television and in films.

Then he said, "I strongly advise you to get into the back of the police car, because if you try any of that monkey business again, you little shit, I will seriously lose my rag. Is that understood?"

I walked over to the police car, which was parked just outside the gate. He opened the back door and I got inside. He climbed into the driver's seat and made a call on his radio to the policewoman, who was still inside the house. He said, "The little bugger just had a pop at me, Kate. Can you hang on with Mrs. S. while I drop him off at the station? I'll get Tony to swing by and pick you up."

And she said, "Sure. I'll catch you later."

The policeman said, "Okeydoke," and we drove off.

The police car smelled of hot plastic and aftershave and take-away chips.

I watched the sky as we drove toward the town center. It was a clear night and you could see the Milky Way.

Some people think the Milky Way is a long line of stars, but it isn't. Our galaxy is a huge disk of stars millions of light-years across, and the solar system is somewhere near the outside edge of the disk.

When you look in direction A, at 90° to the disk, you don't see many stars. But when you look in direction B, you see lots more stars because you are looking into the main body of the galaxy, and because the galaxy is a disk you see a stripe of stars.

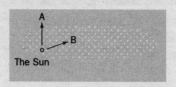

The Sun

And then I thought about how for a long time scientists were puzzled by the fact that the sky is dark at night, even though there are billions of stars in the universe and there must be stars in every direction you look, so that the sky should be full of starlight because there is very little in the way to stop the light from reaching earth.

Then they worked out that the universe was expanding, that the stars were all rushing away from one another after the Big Bang, and the further the stars were away from us the faster they were moving, some of them nearly as fast as the speed of light, which was why their light never reached us.

I like this fact. It is something you can work out in your own mind just by looking at the sky above your head at night and thinking without having to ask anyone.

And when the universe has finished exploding, all the stars will slow down, like a ball that has been thrown into the air, and they will come to a halt and they will all begin to fall toward the center of the universe again. And then there will be nothing to stop us from seeing all the stars in the world because they will all be moving toward us, gradually faster and faster, and we will know that the world is going to end soon because when we look up into the sky at night there will be no darkness, just the blazing light of billions and billions of stars, all falling.

Except that no one will see this because there will be no people left on the earth to see it. They will probably have become extinct by then. And even if there are people still in existence, they will not see it because the light will be so bright and hot that everyone will be burned to death, even if they live in tunnels.

19.   Chapters in books are usually given the cardinal numbers 1, 2, 3, 4, 5, 6 and so on. But I have decided to give my chapters prime numbers 2, 3, 5, 7, 11, 13 and so on because I like prime numbers.

This is how you work out what prime numbers are.

First you write down all the positive whole numbers in the world.

1	2	3	4	5	6	7	8	9	10
11	12	13	14	15	16	17	18	19	20
21	22	23	24	25	26	27	28	29	30
31	32	33	34	35	36	37	38	39	40
41	42	43	44	45	46	47	48	49	etc.

Then you take away all the numbers that are multiples of 2. Then you take away all the numbers that are multiples of 3. Then you take away all the numbers that are multiples of 4 and 5 and 6 and 7 and so on. The numbers that are left are the prime numbers.

	2	3		5		7			
11		13				17		19	
		23						29	
31						37			
41		43				47			etc.

The rule for working out prime numbers is really simple, but no one has ever worked out a simple formula for telling you whether a very big number is a prime number or what the next one will be. If a number is really, really big, it can take a computer years to work out whether it is a prime number.

Prime numbers are useful for writing codes and in America they are classed as Military Material and if you find one over 100 digits long you have to tell the CIA and they buy it off you for $10,000. But it would not be a very good way of making a living.

Prime numbers are what is left when you have taken all the patterns away. I think prime numbers are like life. They are very logical but you could never work out the rules, even if you spent all your time thinking about them.

23. When I got to the police station they made me take the laces out of my shoes and empty my pockets at the front desk in case I had anything in them that I could use to kill myself or escape or attack a policeman with.

The sergeant behind the desk had very hairy hands and he had bitten his nails so much that they had bled.

This is what I had in my pockets

1. A Swiss Army knife with 13 attachments including a wire stripper and a saw and a toothpick and tweezers

2. A piece of string

3. A piece of a wooden puzzle which looked like this

4. 3 pellets of rat food for Toby, my rat

5. £1.47 (this was made up of a £1 coin, a 20p coin, two 10p coins, a 5p coin and a 2p coin)

6. A red paper clip

7. A key for the front door

I was also wearing my watch and they wanted me to leave this at the desk as well but I said that I needed to keep my watch on because I needed to know exactly what time it was. And when they tried to take it off me I screamed, so they let me keep it on.

They asked me if I had any family. I said I did. They asked me who my family was. I said it was Father, but Mother was dead. And I said it was also Uncle Terry, but he was in Sunderland and he was Father's brother, and it was my grandparents, too, but three of them were dead and Grandma Burton was in a home because she had senile dementia and thought that I was someone on television.

Then they asked me for Father's phone number.

I told them that he had two numbers, one for at home and one which was a mobile phone, and I said both of them.

It was nice in the police cell. It was almost a perfect cube, 2 meters long by 2 meters wide by 2 meters high. It contained approximately 8 cubic meters of air. It had a small window with bars and, on the opposite side, a metal door with a long, thin hatch near the floor for sliding trays of food into the cell and a sliding hatch higher up so that policemen could look in and check that prisoners hadn't escaped or committed suicide. There was also a padded bench.

I wondered how I would escape if I was in a story. It would be difficult because the only things I had were my clothes and my shoes, which had no laces in them.

I decided that my best plan would be to wait for a really sunny day and then use my glasses to focus the sunlight on a piece of my clothing and start a fire. I would then make my escape when they saw the smoke and took me out of the cell. And if they didn't notice I would be able to wee on the clothes and put them out.

I wondered whether Mrs. Shears had told the police that I had killed Wellington and whether, when the police found out that she had lied, she would go to prison. Because telling lies about people is called *slander*.

29.   I find people confusing.

This is for two main reasons.

The first main reason is that people do a lot of talking without using any words. Siobhan says that if you raise one eyebrow it can mean lots of different things. It can mean "I want to do sex with you" and it can also mean "I think that what you just said was very stupid."

Siobhan also says that if you close your mouth and breathe out loudly through your nose, it can mean that you are relaxed, or that you are bored, or that you are angry, and it all depends on how much air comes out of your nose and how fast and what shape your mouth is when you do it and how you are sitting and what you said just before and hundreds of other things which are too complicated to work out in a few seconds.

The second main reason is that people often talk using metaphors. These are examples of metaphors

> **I laughed my socks off.**
> **He was the apple of her eye.**
> **They had a skeleton in the cupboard.**
> **We had a real pig of a day.**
> **The dog was stone dead.**

The word *metaphor* means carrying something from one place to another, and it comes from the Greek words μετα (which means *from one place to another*) and φερειν (which means *to carry*), and it is when you describe something by using a word for something that it isn't. This means that the word *metaphor* is a metaphor.

I think it should be called a lie because a pig is not like a day and people do not have skeletons in their cupboards. And when I try and make a picture of the phrase in my head it just confuses me because imagining an apple in someone's eye doesn't have anything to do with liking someone a lot and it makes you forget what the person was talking about.

15

My name is a metaphor. It means *carrying Christ* and it comes from the Greek words χριστος (which means *Jesus Christ*) and φερειν and it was the name given to St. Christopher because he carried Jesus Christ across a river.

This makes you wonder what he was called before he carried Christ across the river. But he wasn't called anything because this is an apocryphal story, which means that it is a lie, too.

Mother used to say that it meant Christopher was a nice name because it was a story about being kind and helpful, but I do not want my name to mean a story about being kind and helpful. I want my name to mean me.

31.   It was 1:12 a.m. when Father arrived at the police station. I did not see him until 1:28 a.m. but I knew he was there because I could hear him.

He was shouting, "I want to see my son," and "Why the hell is he locked up?" and "Of course I'm bloody angry."

Then I heard a policeman telling him to calm down. Then I heard nothing for a long while.

At 1:28 a.m. a policeman opened the door of the cell and told me that there was someone to see me.

I stepped outside. Father was standing in the corridor. He held up his right hand and spread his fingers out in a fan. I held up my left hand and spread my fingers out in a fan and we made our fingers and thumbs touch each other. We do this because sometimes Father wants to give me a hug, but I do not like hugging people so we do this instead, and it means that he loves me.

Then the policeman told us to follow him down the corridor to another room. In the room was a table and three chairs.

He told us to sit down on the far side of the table and he sat down on the other side. There was a tape recorder on the table and I asked whether I was going to be interviewed and he was going to record the interview.

He said, "I don't think there will be any need for that."

He was an inspector. I could tell because he wasn't wearing a uniform. He also had a very hairy nose. It looked as if there were two very small mice hiding in his nostrils.[2]

He said, "I have spoken to your father and he says that you didn't mean to hit the policeman."

I didn't say anything because this wasn't a question.

He said, "Did you mean to hit the policeman?"

I said, "Yes."

He squeezed his face and said, "But you didn't mean to hurt the policeman?"

I thought about this and said, "No. I didn't mean to hurt the policeman. I just wanted him to stop touching me."

Then he said, "You know that it is wrong to hit a policeman, don't you?"

I said, "I do."

He was quiet for a few seconds, then he asked, "Did you kill the dog, Christopher?"

I said, "I didn't kill the dog."

He said, "Do you know that it is wrong to lie to a policeman and that you can get into a very great deal of trouble if you do?"

[2] This is not a *metaphor*, it is a *simile*, which means that it really did look like there were two very small mice hiding in his nostrils, and if you make a picture in your head of a man with two very small mice hiding in his nostrils, you will know what the police inspector looked like. And a simile is not a lie, unless it is a bad simile.

I said, "Yes."

He said, "So, do you know who killed the dog?"

I said, "No."

He said, "Are you telling the truth?"

I said, "Yes. I always tell the truth."

And he said, "Right. I am going to give you a caution."

I asked, "Is that going to be on a piece of paper like a certificate I can keep?"

He replied, "No, a caution means that we are going to keep a record of what you did, that you hit a policeman but that it was an accident and that you didn't mean to hurt the policeman."

I said, "But it wasn't an accident."

And Father said, "Christopher, please."

The policeman closed his mouth and breathed out loudly through his nose and said, "If you get into any more trouble we will take out this record and see that you have been given a caution and we will take things much more seriously. Do you understand what I'm saying?"

I said that I understood.

Then he said that we could go and he stood up and opened the door and we walked out into the corridor and back to the front desk, where I picked up my Swiss Army knife and my piece of string and the piece of the wooden puzzle and the 3 pellets of rat food for Toby and my £1.47 and the paper clip and my front door key, which were all in a little plastic bag, and we went out to Father's car, which was parked outside, and we drove home.

37.   I do not tell lies. Mother used to say that this was because I was a good person. But it is not because I am a good person. It is because I can't tell lies.

Mother was a small person who smelled nice. And she
sometimes wore a fleece with a zip down the front which was
pink and it had a tiny label which said **Berghaus** on the left
bosom.

A lie is when you say something happened which didn't
happen. But there is only ever one thing which happened at a
particular time and a particular place. And there are an infinite
number of things which didn't happen at that time and that
place. And if I think about something which didn't happen I
start thinking about all the other things which didn't happen.

For example, this morning for breakfast I had Ready Brek
and some hot raspberry milk shake. But if I say that I actually
had Shreddies and a mug of tea[5] I start thinking about Coco Pops
and lemonade and porridge and Dr Pepper and how I wasn't eating my breakfast in Egypt and there wasn't a rhinoceros in the
room and Father wasn't wearing a diving suit and so on and even
writing this makes me feel shaky and scared, like I do when I'm
standing on the top of a very tall building and there are thousands of houses and cars and people below me and my head is so
full of all these things that I'm afraid that I'm going to forget to
stand up straight and hang on to the rail and I'm going to fall
over and be killed.

This is another reason why I don't like proper novels, be-

[5] But I wouldn't have Shreddies and tea because they are both brown.

cause they are lies about things which didn't happen and they make me feel shaky and scared.

And this is why everything I have written here is true.

41. There were clouds in the sky on the way home, so I couldn't see the Milky Way.

I said, "I'm sorry," because Father had had to come to the police station, which was a bad thing.

He said, "It's OK."

I said, "I didn't kill the dog."

And he said, "I know."

Then he said, "Christopher, you have to stay out of trouble, OK?"

I said, "I didn't know I was going to get into trouble. I like Wellington and I went to say hello to him, but I didn't know that someone had killed him."

Father said, "Just try and keep your nose out of other people's business."

I thought for a little and I said, "I am going to find out who killed Wellington."

And Father said, "Were you listening to what I was saying, Christopher?"

I said, "Yes, I was listening to what you were saying, but when someone gets murdered you have to find out who did it so that they can be punished."

And he said, "It's a bloody dog, Christopher, a bloody dog."

I replied, "I think dogs are important, too."

He said, "Leave it."

And I said, "I wonder if the police will find out who killed him and punish the person."

Then Father banged the steering wheel with his fist and the car weaved a little bit across the dotted line in the middle of the road and he shouted, "I said leave it, for God's sake."

I could tell that he was angry because he was shouting, and I didn't want to make him angry so I didn't say anything else until we got home.

When we came in through the front door I went into the kitchen and got a carrot for Toby and I went upstairs and I shut the door of my room and I let Toby out and gave him the carrot. Then I turned my computer on and played 76 games of **Minesweeper** and did the Expert Version in 102 seconds, which was only 3 seconds off my best time, which was 99 seconds.

At 2:07 a.m. I decided that I wanted a drink of orange squash before I brushed my teeth and got into bed, so I went downstairs to the kitchen. Father was sitting on the sofa watching snooker on the television and drinking scotch. There were tears coming out of his eyes.

I asked, "Are you sad about Wellington?"

He looked at me for a long time and sucked air in through his nose. Then he said, "Yes, Christopher, you could say that. You could very well say that."

I decided to leave him alone because when I am sad I want to be left alone. So I didn't say anything else. I just went into the kitchen and made my orange squash and took it back upstairs to my room.

43.   Mother died 2 years ago.

I came home from school one day and no one answered the door, so I went and found the secret key that we keep under a flowerpot behind the kitchen door. I let myself into the house and carried on making the Airfix Sherman tank model I was building.

An hour and a half later Father came home from work. He runs a business and he does heating maintenance and boiler repair with a man called Rhodri who is his employee. He knocked on the door of my room and opened it and asked whether I had seen Mother.

I said that I hadn't seen her and he went downstairs and started making some phone calls. I did not hear what he said.

Then he came up to my room and said he had to go out for a while and he wasn't sure how long he would be. He said that if I needed anything I should call him on his mobile phone.

He was away for 2½ hours. When he came back I went downstairs. He was sitting in the kitchen staring out of the back window down the garden to the pond and the corrugated iron fence and the top of the tower of the church on Manstead Street which looks like a castle because it is Norman.

Father said, "I'm afraid you won't be seeing your mother for a while."

He didn't look at me when he said this. He kept on looking through the window.

Usually people look at you when they're talking to you. I know that they're working out what I'm thinking, but I can't tell what they're thinking. It is like being in a room with a one-way mirror in a spy film. But this was nice, having Father speak to me but not look at me.

I said, "Why not?"

He waited for a very long time, then he said, "Your mother has had to go into hospital."

"Can we visit her?" I asked, because I like hospitals. I like the uniforms and the machines.

Father said, "No."

I said, "Why can't we?"

And he said, "She needs rest. She needs to be on her own."

I asked, "Is it a psychiatric hospital?"

And Father said, "No. It's an ordinary hospital. She has a problem . . . a problem with her heart."

I said, "We will need to take food to her," because I knew that food in hospital was not very good. David from school, he went into hospital to have an operation on his leg to make his calf muscle longer so that he could walk better. And he hated the food, so his mother used to take meals in every day.

Father waited for a long time again and said, "I'll take some in to her during the day when you're at school and I'll give it to the doctors and they can give it to your mum, OK?"

I said, "But you can't cook."

Father put his hands over his face and said, "Christopher. Look. I'll buy some ready-made stuff from Marks and Spencer's and take those in. She likes those."

I said I would make her a Get Well card, because that is what you do for people when they are in hospital.

Father said he would take it in the next day.

47.   In the bus on the way to school next morning we passed 4 red cars in a row, which meant that it was a **Good Day,** so I decided not to be sad about Wellington.

Mr. Jeavons, the psychologist at the school, once asked me why 4 red cars in a row made it a **Good Day,** and 3 red cars in a row made it a **Quite Good Day,** and 5 red cars in a row made it a **Super Good Day,** and why 4 yellow cars in a row made it a **Black Day,** which is a day when I don't speak to anyone and sit on my own reading books and don't eat my lunch and *Take No Risks.* He said that I was clearly a very logical person, so he was surprised that I should think like this because it wasn't very logical.

I said that I liked things to be in a nice order. And one way of things being in a nice order was to be logical. Especially if those things were numbers or an argument. But there were other ways of putting things in a nice order. And that was why I had **Good Days** and **Black Days.** And I said that some people who worked in an office came out of their house in the morning and saw that the sun was shining and it made them feel happy, or they saw that it was raining and it made them feel sad, but the only difference was the weather and if they worked in an office the weather didn't have anything to do with whether they had a good day or a bad day.

I said that when Father got up in the morning he always put his trousers on before he put his socks on and it wasn't logical but he always did it that way, because he liked things in a nice order, too. Also whenever he went upstairs he went up two at a time, always starting with his right foot.

Mr. Jeavons said that I was a very clever boy.

I said that I wasn't clever. I was just noticing how things were, and that wasn't clever. That was just being observant. Being clever was when you looked at how things were and used the evidence to work out something new. Like the universe expanding, or who committed a murder. Or if you see someone's name and you give each letter a value from 1 to 26 (**a = 1, b = 2**, etc.) and you add the numbers up in your head and you find that it makes a prime number, like **Jesus Christ** (151), or **Scooby-Doo** (113), or **Sherlock Holmes** (163), or **Doctor Watson** (167).

Mr. Jeavons asked me whether this made me feel safe, having things always in a nice order, and I said it did.

Then he asked if I didn't like things changing. And I said I wouldn't mind things changing if I became an astronaut, for example, which is one of the biggest changes you can imagine, apart from becoming a girl or dying.

He asked whether I wanted to become an astronaut and I said I did.

He said that it was very difficult to become an astronaut. I said that I knew. You had to become an officer in the air force and you had to take lots of orders and be prepared to kill other human beings, and I couldn't take orders. Also I didn't have 20/20 vision, which you needed to be a pilot. But I said that you could still want something that is very unlikely to happen.

Terry, who is the older brother of Francis, who is at the school, said I would only ever get a job collecting supermarket trollies or cleaning out donkey shit at an animal sanctuary and they didn't let spazzers drive rockets that cost billions of pounds. When I told this to Father he said that Terry was jealous of my being cleverer than him. Which was a stupid thing to think because we weren't in a competition. But Terry is stupid, so *quod erat demonstrandum,* which is Latin for *which is the thing that was going to be proved,* which means *thus it is proved.*

I'm not a spazzer, which means *spastic,* not like Francis, who is a spazzer, and even though I probably won't become an astronaut, I am going to go to university and study mathematics, or physics, or physics and mathematics (which is a Joint Honor School), because I like mathematics and physics and I'm very good at them. But Terry won't go to university. Father says Terry is most likely to end up in prison.

Terry has a tattoo on his arm of a heart shape with a knife through the middle of it.

But this is what is called a digression, and now I am going to go back to the fact that it was a Good Day.

Because it was a Good Day I decided that I would try and find out who killed Wellington because a Good Day is a day for projects and planning things.

When I said this to Siobhan she said, "Well, we're meant to be writing stories today, so why don't you write about finding Wellington and going to the police station."

And that is when I started writing this.

And Siobhan said that she would help with the spelling and the grammar and the footnotes.

53.   Mother died two weeks later.

I had not been into hospital to see her but Father had taken in lots of food from Marks and Spencer's. He said that she had been looking OK and seemed to be getting better. She had sent me lots of love and had my Get Well card on the table beside her bed. Father said that she liked it very much.

The card had pictures of cars on the front. It looked like this

I did it at school with Mrs. Peters, who does art, and it was a lino cut, which is when you draw a picture on a piece of lino and Mrs. Peters cuts round the picture with a Stanley knife and then you put ink on the lino and press it onto the paper, which is why all the cars looked the same, because I did one car and pressed it onto the paper 9 times. And it was Mrs. Peters's idea to do lots of cars, which I liked. And I colored all the cars in with red paint to make it a **Super Super Good Day** for Mother.

Father said that she died of a heart attack and it wasn't expected.

I said, "What kind of heart attack?" because I was surprised.

Mother was only 38 years old and heart attacks usually happen to older people, and Mother was very active and rode a bicycle and ate food which was healthy and high in fiber and low in saturated fat like chicken and vegetables and muesli.

Father said that he didn't know what kind of heart attack she had and now wasn't the moment to be asking questions like that.

I said that it was probably an aneurysm.

A heart attack is when some of the muscles in the heart stop getting blood and die. There are two main types of heart attack. The first is an embolism. That is when a blood clot blocks one of the blood vessels taking blood to the muscles in the heart.

And you can stop this from happening by taking aspirin and eating fish. Which is why Eskimos don't get this sort of heart attack, because they eat fish and fish stops their blood from clotting, but if they cut themselves badly they can bleed to death.

But an aneurysm is when a blood vessel breaks and the blood doesn't get to the heart muscles because it is leaking. And some people get aneurysms just because there is a weak bit in their blood vessels, like Mrs. Hardisty, who lived at number 72 in our street, who had a weak bit in the blood vessels in her neck and died just because she turned her head round to reverse her car into a parking space.

On the other hand, it could have been an embolism, because your blood clots much more easily when you are lying down for a long time, like when you are in hospital.

Father said, "I'm sorry, Christopher, I'm really sorry."

But it wasn't his fault.

Then Mrs. Shears came over and cooked supper for us. And she was wearing sandals and jeans and a T-shirt which had the words **WINDSURF** and **CORFU** and a picture of a windsurfer on it.

And Father was sitting down and she stood next to him and held his head against her bosoms and said, "Come on, Ed. We're going to get you through this."

And then she made us spaghetti and tomato sauce.

And after dinner she played Scrabble with me and I beat her 247 points to 134.

59.   I decided that I was going to find out who killed Wellington even though Father had told me to stay out of other people's business.

This is because I do not always do what I am told.

And this is because when people tell you what to do it is usually confusing and does not make sense.

For example, people often say "Be quiet," but they don't tell you how long to be quiet for. Or you see a sign which says **KEEP OFF THE GRASS** but it should say **KEEP OFF THE GRASS AROUND THIS SIGN** or **KEEP OFF ALL THE GRASS IN THIS PARK** because there is lots of grass you are allowed to walk on.

Also people break rules all the time. For example, Father often drives at over 30 mph in a 30 mph zone and sometimes he drives when he has been drinking and often he doesn't wear his seat belt when he is driving his van. And in the Bible it says *Thou shalt not kill* but there were the Crusades and two world wars and the Gulf War and there were Christians killing people in all of them.

Also I don't know what Father means when he says "Stay out of other people's business" because I do not know what he means by "other people's business" because I do lots of things with other people, at school and in the shop and on the bus, and his job is going into other people's houses and fixing their boilers and their heating. And all of these things are other people's business.

Siobhan understands. When she tells me not to do something she tells me exactly what it is that I am not allowed to do. And I like this.

For example, she once said, "You must never punch Sarah or hit her in any way, Christopher. Even if she hits you first. If she does hit you again, move away from her and stand still and count from 1 to 50, then come and tell me what she has done, or tell one of the other members of staff what she has done."

Or, for example, she once said, "If you want to go on the

swings and there are already people on the swings, you must never push them off. You must ask them if you can have a go. And then you must wait until they have finished."

But when other people tell you what you can't do they don't do it like this. So I decide for myself what I am going to do and what I am not going to do.

That evening I went round to Mrs. Shears's house and knocked on the door and waited for her to answer it.

When she opened the door she was holding a mug of tea and she was wearing sheepskin slippers and she had been watching a quiz program on the television because there was a television on and I could hear someone saying, "The capital city of Venezuela is . . . (a) Maracas, (b) Caracas, (c) Bogotá or (d) Georgetown." And I knew that it was Caracas.

She said, "Christopher, I really don't think I want to see you right now."

I said, "I didn't kill Wellington."

And she replied, "What are you doing here?"

I said, "I wanted to come and tell you that I didn't kill Wellington. And also I want to find out who killed him."

Some of her tea spilled onto the carpet.

I said, "Do you know who killed Wellington?"

She didn't answer my question. She just said, "Goodbye, Christopher," and closed the door.

Then I decided to do some detective work.

I could see that she was watching me and waiting for me to leave because I could see her standing in her hall on the other side of the frosted glass in her front door. So I walked down the path and out of the garden. Then I turned round and saw that she wasn't standing in her hall any longer. I made sure that there was no one watching and climbed over the wall and walked down the side of the house into her back garden to the shed where she kept all her gardening tools.

The shed was locked with a padlock and I couldn't go inside so I walked round to the window in the side. Then I had some good luck. When I looked through the window I could see a fork that looked exactly the same as the fork that had been sticking out of Wellington. It was lying on the bench by the window and it had been cleaned because there was no blood on the spikes. I could see some other tools as well, a spade and a rake and one of those long clippers people use for cutting branches which are too high to reach. And they all had the same green plastic handles like the fork. This meant that the fork belonged to Mrs. Shears. Either that or it was a *Red Herring*, which is a clue which makes you come to a wrong conclusion or something which looks like a clue but isn't.

I wondered if Mrs. Shears had killed Wellington herself. But if she had killed Wellington herself, why had she come out of the house shouting, "What in fuck's name have you done to my dog?"

I thought that Mrs. Shears probably didn't kill Wellington. But whoever had killed him had probably killed him with Mrs. Shears's fork. And the shed was locked. This meant that it was someone who had the key to Mrs. Shears's shed, or that she had left it unlocked, or that she had left her fork lying around in the garden.

I heard a noise and turned round and saw Mrs. Shears standing on the lawn looking at me.

I said, "I came to see if the fork was in the shed."

And she said, "If you don't go now I will call the police again."

So I went home.

When I got home I said hello to Father and went upstairs and fed Toby, my rat, and felt happy because I was being a detective and finding things out.

61.   Mrs. Forbes at school said that when Mother died she had gone to heaven. That was because Mrs. Forbes is very old and she believes in heaven. And she wears tracksuit trousers because she says that they are more comfortable than normal trousers. And one of her legs is very slightly shorter than the other one because of an accident on a motorbike.

But when Mother died she didn't go to heaven because heaven doesn't exist.

Mrs. Peters's husband is a vicar called the Reverend Peters, and he comes to our school sometimes to talk to us, and I asked him where heaven was and he said, "It's not in our universe. It's another kind of place altogether."

The Reverend Peters makes a funny ticking noise with his tongue sometimes when he is thinking. And he smokes cigarettes and you can smell them on his breath and I don't like this.

I said that there wasn't anything outside the universe and there wasn't another kind of place altogether. Except that there might be if you went through a black hole, but a black hole is what is called a *singularity*, which means it is impossible to find out what is on the other side because the gravity of a black hole is so big that even electromagnetic waves like light can't get out of it, and electromagnetic waves are how we get information about things which are far away. And if heaven was on the other side of a black hole, dead people would have to be fired into space on rockets to get there, and they aren't or people would notice.

I think people believe in heaven because they don't like the idea of dying, because they want to carry on living and they don't like the idea that other people will move into their house and put their things into the rubbish.

The Reverend Peters said, "Well, when I say that heaven is outside the universe it's really just a manner of speaking. I suppose what it really means is that they are with God."

And I replied, "But where is God?"

And the Reverend Peters said that we should talk about this on another day when he had more time.

What actually happens when you die is that your brain stops working and your body rots, like Rabbit did when he died and we buried him in the earth at the bottom of the garden. And all his molecules were broken down into other molecules and they went into the earth and were eaten by worms and went into the plants and if we go and dig in the same place in 10 years there will be nothing except his skeleton left. And in 1,000 years even his skeleton will be gone. But that is all right because he is a part of the flowers and the apple tree and the hawthorn bush now.

When people die they are sometimes put into coffins, which means that they don't mix with the earth for a very long time until the wood of the coffin rots.

But Mother was cremated. This means that she was put into a coffin and burned and ground up and turned into ash and smoke. I do not know what happens to the ash and I couldn't ask at the crematorium because I didn't go to the funeral. But the smoke goes out of the chimney and into the air and sometimes I look up into the sky and I think that there are molecules of

Mother up there, or in clouds over Africa or the Antarctic, or coming down as rain in the rain forests in Brazil, or in snow somewhere.

6 7. The next day was Saturday and there is not much to do on a Saturday unless Father takes me out somewhere on an outing to the boating lake or to the garden center, but on this Saturday England were playing Romania at football, which meant that we weren't going to go on an outing because Father wanted to watch the match on the television. So I decided to do some more detection on my own.

I decided that I would go and ask some of the other people who lived in our street if they had seen anyone killing Wellington or whether they had seen anything strange happening in the street on Thursday night.

Talking to strangers is not something I usually do. I do not like talking to strangers. This is not because of **Stranger Danger,** which they tell us about at school, which is where a strange man offers you sweets or a ride in his car because he wants to do sex with you. I am not worried about that. If a strange man touched me I would hit him, and I can hit people very hard. For example, when I punched Sarah because she had pulled my hair I knocked her unconscious and she had concussion and they had to take her to the Accident and Emergency Department at the hospital. And also I always have my Swiss Army knife in my pocket and it has a saw blade which could cut a man's fingers off.

I do not like strangers because I do not like people I have never met before. They are hard to understand. It is like being in France, which is where we went on holiday sometimes when

3 4

Mother was alive, to camp. And I hated it because if you went into a shop or a restaurant or on a beach you couldn't understand what anyone was saying, which was frightening.

It takes me a long time to get used to people I do not know. For example, when there is a new member of staff at school I do not talk to them for weeks and weeks. I just watch them until I know that they are safe. Then I ask them questions about themselves, like whether they have pets and what is their favorite color and what do they know about the Apollo space missions and I get them to draw a plan of their house and I ask them what kind of car they drive, so I get to know them. Then I don't mind if I am in the same room as them and don't have to watch them all the time.

So talking to the other people in our street was brave. But if you are going to do detective work you have to be brave, so I had no choice.

First of all I made a plan of our part of the street, which is called Randolph Street, like this

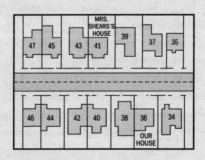

Then I made sure I had my Swiss Army knife in my pocket and I went out and I knocked on the door of number 40, which is opposite Mrs. Shears's house, which means that they were

most likely to have seen something. The people who live at number 40 are called Thompson.

Mr. Thompson answered the door. He was wearing a T-shirt which said

BEER
Helping ugly people
have sex for 2,000 years

Mr. Thompson said, "Can I help you?"

I said, "Do you know who killed Wellington?"

I did not look at his face. I do not like looking at people's faces, especially if they are strangers. He did not say anything for a few seconds.

Then he said, "Who are you?"

I said, "I'm Christopher Boone from number 36 and I know you. You're Mr. Thompson."

He said, "I'm Mr. Thompson's brother."

I said, "Do you know who killed Wellington?"

He said, "Who the fuck is Wellington?"

I said, "Mrs. Shears's dog. Mrs. Shears is from number 41."

He said, "Someone killed her dog?"

I said, "With a fork."

He said, "Jesus Christ."

I said, "A garden fork," in case he thought I meant a fork you eat your food with. Then I said, "Do you know who killed him?"

He said, "I haven't a bloody clue."

I said, "Did you see anything suspicious on Thursday evening?"

He said, "Look, son, do you really think you should be going around asking questions like this?"

And I said, "Yes, because I want to find out who killed Wellington, and I am writing a book about it."

And he said, "Well, I was in Colchester on Thursday, so you're asking the wrong bloke."

I said, "Thank you," and I walked away.

There was no answer at house number 42.

I had seen the people who lived at number 44, but I did not know what their names were. They were black people and they were a man and a lady with two children, a boy and a girl. The lady answered the door. She was wearing boots which looked like army boots and there were 5 bracelets made out of a silver-colored metal on her wrist and they made a jangling noise. She said, "It's Christopher, isn't it."

I said that it was, and I asked her if she knew who killed Wellington. She knew who Wellington was so I didn't have to explain, and she had heard about him being killed.

I asked if she had seen anything suspicious on Thursday evening which might be a clue.

She said, "Like what?"

And I said, "Like strangers. Or like the sound of people arguing."

But she said she hadn't.

And then I decided to do what is called *Trying a Different Tack*, and I asked her whether she knew of anyone who might want to make Mrs. Shears sad.

And she said, "Perhaps you should be talking to your father about this."

And I explained that I couldn't ask my father because the

investigation was a secret because he had told me to stay out of other people's business.

She said, "Well, maybe he has a point, Christopher."

And I said, "So, you don't know anything which might be a clue."

And she said, "No," and then she said, "You be careful, young man."

I said that I would be careful and then I said thank you to her for helping me with my questions and I went to number 43, which is the house next to Mrs. Shears's house.

The people who live at number 43 are Mr. Wise and Mr. Wise's mother, who is in a wheelchair, which is why he lives with her, so he can take her to the shops and drive her around.

It was Mr. Wise who answered the door. He smelled of body odor and old biscuits and off popcorn, which is what you smell of if you haven't washed for a very long time, like Jason at school smells because his family is poor.

I asked Mr. Wise if he knew who had killed Wellington on Thursday night.

He said, "Bloody hell, policemen really are getting younger, aren't they."

Then he laughed. I do not like people laughing at me, so I turned and walked away.

I did not knock at the door of number 38, which is the house next to our house, because the people there take drugs and Father says that I should never talk to them, so I don't. And they play loud music at night and they make me scared sometimes when I see them in the street. And it is not really their house.

Then I noticed that the old lady who lives at number 39, which is on the other side of Mrs. Shears's house, was in her front garden cutting her hedge with an electric hedge trimmer.

Her name is Mrs. Alexander. She has a dog. It is a dachshund, so she was probably a good person because she liked dogs. But the dog wasn't in the garden with her. It was inside the house.

Mrs. Alexander was wearing jeans and training shoes, which old people don't normally wear. And there was mud on the jeans. And the trainers were New Balance trainers. And the laces were red.

I went up to Mrs. Alexander and said, "Do you know anything about Wellington being killed?"

Then she turned the electric hedge trimmer off and said, "I'm afraid you're going to have to say that again. I'm a little deaf."

So I said, "Do you know anything about Wellington being killed?"

And she said, "I heard about it yesterday. Dreadful. Dreadful."

I said, "Do you know who killed him?"

And she said, "No, I don't."

I replied, "Somebody must know because the person who killed Wellington knows that they killed Wellington. Unless they were a mad person and didn't know what they were doing. Or unless they had amnesia."

And she said, "Well, I suppose you're probably right."

I said, "Thank you for helping me with my investigation."

And she said, "You're Christopher, aren't you."

I said, "Yes. I live at number 36."

And she said, "We haven't talked before, have we."

I said, "No. I don't like talking to strangers. But I'm doing detective work."

And she said, "I see you every day, going to school."

I didn't reply to this.

And she said, "It's very nice of you to come and say hello."

I didn't reply to this either because Mrs. Alexander was doing what is called chatting, where people say things to each other which aren't questions and answers and aren't connected.

Then she said, "Even if it's only because you're doing detective work."

And I said, "Thank you" again.

And I was about to turn and walk away when she said, "I have a grandson your age."

I tried to do chatting by saying, "My age is 15 years and 3 months and 3 days."

And she said, "Well, almost your age."

Then we said nothing for a little while until she said, "You don't have a dog, do you?"

And I said, "No."

She said, "You'd probably like a dog, wouldn't you."

And I said, "I have a rat."

And she said, "A rat?"

And I said, "He's called Toby."

And she said, "Oh."

And I said, "Most people don't like rats because they think they carry diseases like bubonic plague. But that's only because they lived in sewers and stowed away on ships coming from foreign countries where there were strange diseases. But rats are very clean. Toby is always washing himself. And you don't have to take him out for walks. I just let him run around my room so that he gets some exercise. And sometimes he sits on my shoulder or hides in my sleeve like it's a burrow. But rats don't live in burrows in nature."

Mrs. Alexander said, "Do you want to come in for tea?"

And I said, "I don't go into other people's houses."

And she said, "Well, maybe I could bring some out here. Do you like lemon squash?"

I replied, "I only like orange squash."

And she said, "Luckily I have some of that as well. And what about Battenberg?"

And I said, "I don't know because I don't know what Battenberg is."

She said, "It's a kind of cake. It has four pink and yellow squares in the middle and it has marzipan icing round the edge."

And I said, "Is it a long cake with a square cross section which is divided into equally sized, alternately colored squares?"

And she said, "Yes, I think you could probably describe it like that."

I said, "I think I'd like the pink squares but not the yellow squares because I don't like yellow. And I don't know what marzipan is, so I don't know whether I'd like that."

And she said, "I'm afraid marzipan is yellow, too. Perhaps I should bring out some biscuits instead. Do you like biscuits?"

And I said, "Yes. Some sorts of biscuits."

And she said, "I'll get a selection."

Then she turned and went into the house. She moved very slowly because she was an old lady and she was inside the house for more than 6 minutes and I began to get nervous because I didn't know what she was doing in the house. I didn't know her well enough to know whether she was telling the truth about getting orange squash and Battenberg cake. And I thought she might be ringing the police and then I'd get into much more serious trouble because of the caution.

So I walked away.

And as I was crossing the street I had a stroke of inspiration about who might have killed Wellington. I was imagining a Chain of Reasoning inside my head which was like this

    1. Why would you kill a dog?

      a) Because you hated the dog.

      b) Because you were mad.

      c) Because you wanted to make Mrs. Shears upset.

    2. I didn't know anyone who hated Wellington, so if it was **(a)** it was probably a stranger.

    3. I didn't know any mad people, so if it was **(b)** it was also probably a stranger.

    4. Most murders are committed by someone who is known to the victim. In fact, you are most likely to be murdered by a member of your own family on Christmas Day. This is a fact. Wellington was therefore most likely to have been killed by someone known to him.

    5. If it was **(c)** I only knew one person who didn't like Mrs. Shears, and that was Mr. Shears, who knew Wellington very well indeed.

This meant that Mr. Shears was my **Prime Suspect.**

Mr. Shears used to be married to Mrs. Shears and they lived together until two years ago. Then Mr. Shears left and didn't come back. This was why Mrs. Shears came over and did lots of cooking for us after Mother died, because she didn't have to cook for Mr. Shears anymore and she didn't have to stay at home and be his wife. And also Father said that she needed company and didn't want to be on her own.

And sometimes Mrs. Shears stayed overnight at our house and I liked it when she did because she made things tidy and she arranged the jars and pans and tins in order of their height on the shelves in the kitchen and she always made their labels face outward and she put the knives and forks and spoons in the correct compartments in the cutlery drawer. But she smoked cigarettes and she said lots of things I didn't understand, e.g., "I'm going to hit the hay," and "It's brass monkeys out there," and "Let's rustle up some tucker." And I didn't like when she said things like that because I didn't know what she meant.

And I don't know why Mr. Shears left Mrs. Shears because nobody told me. But when you get married it is because you want to live together and have children, and if you get married in a church you have to promise that you will stay together until death do us part. And if you don't want to live together you have to get divorced and this is because one of you has done sex with somebody else or because you are having arguments and you hate each other and you don't want to live in the same house anymore and have children. And Mr. Shears didn't want to live in the same house as Mrs. Shears anymore so he probably hated her and he might have come back and killed her dog to make her sad.

I decided to try and find out more about Mr. Shears.

71.   All the other children at my school are stupid. Except I'm not meant to call them stupid, even though this is what they are. I'm meant to say that they have learning difficulties or that they have special needs. But this is stupid because everyone has learning difficulties because learning to speak French or understanding relativity is difficult and also everyone has special needs, like Father, who has to carry a little packet of artificial sweetening tablets around with him to put in his coffee to stop him from getting fat, or Mrs. Peters, who wears a beige-colored hearing aid, or Siobhan, who has glasses so thick that they give you a headache if you borrow them, and none of these people are Special Needs, even if they have special needs.

But Siobhan said we have to use those words because people used to call children like the children at school *spaz* and *crip* and *mong*, which were nasty words. But that is stupid too because sometimes the children from the school down the road see us in the street when we're getting off the bus and they shout, "Special Needs! Special Needs!" But I don't take any notice because I don't listen to what other people say and only sticks and stones can break my bones and I have my Swiss Army knife if they hit me and if I kill them it will be self-defense and I won't go to prison.

I am going to prove that I'm not stupid. Next month I'm going to take my A level in maths and I'm going to get an A grade. No one has ever taken an A level at our school before, and the headmistress, Mrs. Gascoyne, didn't want me to take it at first. She said they didn't have the facilities to let us sit A levels. But Father had an argument with Mrs. Gascoyne and he got really cross. Mrs. Gascoyne said they didn't want to treat me differently from everyone else in the school because then everyone would want to be treated differently and it would set a precedent. And I could always do my A levels later, at 18.

I was sitting in Mrs. Gascoyne's office with Father when she said these things. And Father said, "Christopher is getting a crap enough deal already, don't you think, without you shitting on him from a great height as well. Jesus, this is the one thing he is really good at."

Then Mrs. Gascoyne said that she and Father should talk about this at some later point on their own. But Father asked her whether she wanted to say things she was embarrassed to say in front of me, and she said no, so he said, "Say them now, then."

And she said that if I sat an A level I would have to have a member of staff looking after me on my own in a separate room. And Father said he would pay someone £50 to do it after school and he wasn't going to take no for an answer. And she said she'd go away and think about it. And the next week she rang Father at home and told him that I could take the A level and the Reverend Peters would be what is called the invigilator.

And after I've taken A-level maths I am going to take A-level further maths and physics and then I can go to university. There is not a university in our town, which is Swindon, because it is a small place. So we will have to move to another town where there is a university because I don't want to live on my own or in a house with other students. But that will be all right because Father wants to move to a different town as well. He sometimes say things like, "We've got to get out of this town, kiddo." And sometimes he says, "Swindon is the arsehole of the world."

Then, when I've got a degree in maths, or physics, or maths and physics, I will be able to get a job and earn lots of money and I will be able to pay someone who can look after me and cook my meals and wash my clothes, or I will get a lady to marry me and be my wife and she can look after me so I can have company and not be on my own.

73. I used to think that Mother and Father might get divorced. That was because they had lots of arguments and sometimes they hated each other. This was because of the stress of looking after someone who has Behavioral Problems like I have. I used to have lots of Behavioral Problems, but I don't have so many now because I'm more grown up and I can take decisions for myself and do things on my own like going out of the house and buying things at the shop at the end of the road.

These are some of my Behavioral Problems

A. Not talking to people for a long time[4]

B. Not eating or drinking anything for a long time[5]

C. Not liking being touched

D. Screaming when I am angry or confused

E. Not liking being in really small places with other people

F. Smashing things when I am angry or confused

G. Groaning

H. Not liking yellow things or brown things and refusing to touch yellow things or brown things

I. Refusing to use my toothbrush if anyone else has touched it

J. Not eating food if different sorts of food are touching each other

K. Not noticing that people are angry with me

L. Not smiling

M. Saying things that other people think are rude[6]

---

[4] Once I didn't talk to anyone for 5 weeks.

[5] When I was 6 Mother used to get me to drink strawberry-flavored slimming meals out of a measuring jug and we would have competitions to see how fast I could drink a quarter of a liter.

[6] People say that you always have to tell the truth. But they do not mean this because you are not allowed to tell old people that they are old and you are

N. Doing stupid things[7]

O. Hitting other people

P. Hating France

Q. Driving Mother's car[8]

R. Getting cross when someone has moved the furniture[9]

Sometimes these things would make Mother and Father really angry and they would shout at me or they would shout at each other. Sometimes Father would say, "Christopher, if you do not behave I swear I shall knock the living daylights out of you,"

———

not allowed to tell people if they smell funny or if a grown-up has made a fart. And you are not allowed to say "I don't like you" unless that person has been horrible to you.

[7] Stupid things are things like emptying a jar of peanut butter onto the table in the kitchen and making it level with a knife so it covers all the table right to the edges, or burning things on the gas stove to see what happened to them, like my shoes or silver foil or sugar.

[8] I only did this once by borrowing the keys when she went into town on the bus, and I hadn't driven a car before and I was 8 years old and 5 months so I drove it into the wall, and the car isn't there anymore because Mother is dead.

[9] It is permitted to move the chairs and the table in the kitchen because that is different, but it makes me feel dizzy and sick if someone has moved the sofa and the chairs around in the living room or the dining room. Mother used to do this when she did the hoovering, so I made a special plan of where all the furniture was meant to be and did measurements and I put everything back in its proper place afterward and then I felt better. But since Mother died Father hasn't done any hoovering, so that is OK. And Mrs. Shears did the hoovering once but I did groaning and she shouted at Father and she never did it again.

or Mother would say, "Jesus, Christopher, I am seriously considering putting you in a home," or Mother would say, "You are going to drive me into an early grave."

79. When I got home Father was sitting at the table in the kitchen and he had made my supper. He was wearing a lumberjack shirt. The supper was baked beans and broccoli and two slices of ham and they were laid out on the plate so that they were not touching.

He said, "Where have you been?"

And I said, "I have been out." This is called a white lie. A white lie is not a lie at all. It is where you tell the truth but you do not tell all of the truth. This means that everything you say is a white lie because when someone says, for example, "What do you want to do today?" you say, "I want to do painting with Mrs. Peters," but you don't say, "I want to have my lunch and I want to go to the toilet and I want to go home after school and I want to play with Toby and I want to have my supper and I want to play on my computer and I want to go to bed." And I said a white lie because I knew that Father didn't want me to be a detective.

Father said, "I have just had a phone call from Mrs. Shears."

I started eating my baked beans and broccoli and two slices of ham.

Then Father asked, "What the hell were you doing poking round her garden?"

I said, "I was doing detective work trying to find out who killed Wellington."

Father replied, "How many times do I have to tell you, Christopher?"

The baked beans and the broccoli and the ham were cold but I didn't mind this. I eat very slowly so my food is nearly always cold.

Father said, "I told you to keep your nose out of other people's business."

I said, "I think Mr. Shears probably killed Wellington."

Father didn't say anything.

I said, "He is my Prime Suspect. Because I think someone might have killed Wellington to make Mrs. Shears sad. And a murder is usually committed by someone known—"

Father banged the table with his fist really hard so that the plates and his knife and fork jumped around and my ham jumped sideways so that it touched the broccoli, so I couldn't eat the ham or the broccoli anymore.

Then he shouted, "I will not have that man's name mentioned in my house."

I asked, "Why not?"

And he said, "That man is evil."

And I said, "Does that mean he might have killed Wellington?"

Father put his head in his hands and said, "Jesus wept."

I could see that Father was angry with me, so I said, "I know you told me not to get involved in other people's business but Mrs. Shears is a friend of ours."

And Father said, "Well, she's not a friend anymore."

And I asked, "Why not?"

And Father said, "OK, Christopher. I am going to say this for the last and final time. I will not tell you again. Look at me when I'm talking to you, for God's sake. Look at me. You are not to go asking Mrs. Shears about who killed that bloody dog. You are not to go asking anyone about who killed that bloody dog. You are not to go trespassing in other people's gardens. You are to stop this ridiculous bloody detective game right now."

I didn't say anything.

Father said, "I am going to make you promise, Christopher. And you know what it means when I make you promise."

I did know what it meant when you say you promise something. You have to say that you will never do something again and then you must never do it because that would make the promise a lie. I said, "I know."

Father said, "Promise me you will stop doing these things. Promise that you will give up this ridiculous game right now, OK?"

I said, "I promise."

83. I think I would make a very good astronaut.

To be a good astronaut you have to be intelligent and I'm intelligent. You also have to understand how machines work and I'm good at understanding how machines work. You also have to be someone who would like being on their own in a tiny spacecraft thousands and thousands of miles away from the surface of the earth and not panic or get claustrophobia or homesick or insane. And I like really little spaces, so long as there is no one else in them with me. Sometimes when I want to be on my own I get into the airing cupboard outside the bathroom and slide in beside the boiler and pull the door closed behind me and sit there and think for hours and it makes me feel very calm.

So I would have to be an astronaut on my own, or have my own part of the spacecraft which no one else could come into.

And also there are no yellow things or brown things in a spacecraft, so that would be OK, too.

And I would have to talk to other people from Mission Control, but we would do that through a radio linkup and a TV monitor, so they wouldn't be like real people who are strangers, but it would be like playing a computer game.

Also I wouldn't be homesick at all because I'd be surrounded by lots of the things I like, which are machines and computers and outer space. And I would be able to look out of a little window in the spacecraft and know that there was no one else near me for thousands and thousands of miles, which is what I sometimes pretend at night in the summer when I go and lie on the lawn and look up at the sky and I put my hands round the sides of my face so that I can't see the fence and the chimney and the washing line and I can pretend I'm in space.

And all I could see would be stars. And stars are the places where the molecules that life is made of were constructed billions of years ago. For example, all the iron in your blood which stops you from being anemic was made in a star.

And I would like it if I could take Toby with me into space, and that might be allowed because they sometimes do take animals into space for experiments, so if I could think of a good experiment you could do with a rat that didn't hurt the rat, I could make them let me take Toby.

But if they didn't let me I would still go because it would be a Dream Come True.

89. The next day at school I told Siobhan that Father had told me I couldn't do any more detecting, which meant that the book was finished. I showed her the pages I had written so far, with the diagram of the universe and the map of the street and the prime numbers. And she said that it didn't matter. She said the book was really good as it was and that I should be very proud of having written a book at all, even if it was quite short and there were some very good books which were very short like *Heart of Darkness,* which was by Conrad.

But I said that it wasn't a proper book because it didn't have a proper ending because I never found out who killed Wellington so the murderer was still At Large.

And she said that was like life, and not all murders were solved and not all murderers were caught. Like Jack the Ripper.

I said I didn't like the idea that the murderer was still At Large. I said I didn't like to think that the person who killed Wellington could be living somewhere nearby and I might meet him when I went out for a walk at night. And this was possible because a murder was usually committed by a person who was known to the victim.

Then I said, "Father said I was never to mention Mr. Shears's name in our house again and that he was an evil man and maybe that meant he was the person who killed Wellington."

And she said, "Perhaps your father just doesn't like Mr. Shears very much."

And I asked, "Why?"

And she said, "I don't know, Christopher. I don't know because I don't know anything about Mr. Shears."

I said, "Mr. Shears used to be married to Mrs. Shears and he left her, like in a divorce. But I don't know if they were actually divorced."

And Siobhan said, "Well, Mrs. Shears is a friend of yours, isn't she. A friend of you and your father. So perhaps your father doesn't like Mr. Shears because he left Mrs. Shears. Because he did something bad to someone who is a friend."

And I said, "But Father says Mrs. Shears isn't a friend of ours anymore."

And Siobhan said, "I'm sorry, Christopher. I wish I could answer all these questions, but I simply don't know."

Then the bell went for the end of school.

The next day I saw 4 yellow cars in a row on the way to school, which made it a **Black Day,** so I didn't eat anything at lunch and I sat in the corner of the room all day and read my A-level maths course book. And the next day, too, I saw 4 yellow cars in a row on the way to school, which made it another **Black Day** too, so I didn't speak to anyone and for the whole afternoon I sat in the corner of the Library groaning with my head pressed into the join between the two walls and this made me feel calm and safe. But on the third day I kept my eyes closed all the way to school until we got off the bus because after I have had 2 **Black Days** in a row I'm allowed to do that.

97.   But it wasn't the end of the book because five days later I saw 5 red cars in a row, which made it a **Super Good Day,** and I knew that something special was going to happen. Nothing special happened at school so I knew something special was going to happen after school. And when I got home I went down to the shop at the end of our road to buy some licorice laces and a Milky Bar with my pocket money.

And when I had bought my licorice laces and a Milky Bar I turned round and saw Mrs. Alexander, the old lady from number 39, who was in the shop as well. She wasn't wearing jeans now. She was wearing a dress like a normal old lady. And she smelled of cooking.

She said, "What happened to you the other day?"

I asked, "Which day?"

And she said, "I came out again and you'd gone. I had to eat all the biscuits myself."

I said, "I went away."

And she said, "I gathered that."

I said, "I thought you might ring the police."

And she said, "Why on earth would I do that?"

And I said, "Because I was poking my nose into other people's business and Father said I shouldn't investigate who killed Wellington. And a policeman gave me a caution and if I get into trouble again it will be a lot worse because of the caution."

Then the Indian lady behind the counter said to Mrs. Alexander, "Can I help you?" and Mrs. Alexander said she'd like a pint of milk and a packet of Jaffa cakes and I went out of the shop.

When I was outside the shop I saw that Mrs. Alexander's dachshund was sitting on the pavement. It was wearing a little coat made out of tartan material, which is Scottish and check. She had tied its lead to the drainpipe next to the door. I like dogs, so I bent down and I said hello to her dog and it licked my hand. Its tongue was rough and wet and it liked the smell on my trousers and started sniffing them.

Then Mrs. Alexander came outside and said, "His name is Ivor."

I didn't say anything.

And Mrs. Alexander said, "You're very shy, aren't you, Christopher."

And I said, "I'm not allowed to talk to you."

And she said, "Don't worry. I'm not going to tell the police and I'm not going to tell your father, because there's nothing wrong with having a chat. Having a chat is just being friendly, isn't it."

I said, "I can't do chatting."

Then she said, "Do you like computers?"

And I said, "Yes. I like computers. I have a computer at home in my bedroom."

And she said, "I know. I can see you sitting at your computer in your bedroom sometimes when I look across the street."

Then she untied Ivor's lead from the drainpipe.

I wasn't going to say anything because I didn't want to get into trouble.

Then I thought that this was a **Super Good Day** and something special hadn't happened yet, so it was possible that talking to Mrs. Alexander was the special thing that was going to happen. And I thought that she might tell me something about Wellington or about Mr. Shears without me asking her, so that wouldn't be breaking my promise.

So I said, "And I like maths and looking after Toby. And also I like outer space and I like being on my own."

And she said, "I bet you're very good at maths, aren't you."

And I said, "I am. I'm going to do my A-level maths next month. And I'm going to get an A grade."

And Mrs. Alexander said, "Really? A-level maths?"

I replied, "Yes. I don't tell lies."

And she said, "I apologize. I didn't mean to suggest that you were lying. I just wondered if I heard you correctly. I'm a little deaf sometimes."

And I said, "I remember. You told me." And then I said, "I'm the first person to do an A level from my school because it's a special school."

And she said, "Well, I am very impressed. And I hope you do get an A."

And I said, "I will."

Then she said, "And the other thing I know about you is that your favorite color is not yellow."

And I said, "No. And it's not brown either. My favorite color is red. And metal color."

Then Ivor did a poo and Mrs. Alexander picked it up with her hand inside a little plastic bag and then she turned the plastic bag inside out and tied a knot in the top so that the poo was all sealed up and she didn't touch the poo with her hands.

And then I did some reasoning. I reasoned that Father had only made me do a promise about five things, which were

1. Not to mention Mr. Shears's name in our house
2. Not to go asking Mrs. Shears about who killed that bloody dog
3. Not to go asking anyone about who killed that bloody dog
4. Not to go trespassing in other people's gardens
5. To stop this ridiculous bloody detective game

And asking about Mr. Shears wasn't any of these things.

And if you are a detective you have to *Take Risks*, and this was a
Super Good Day, which meant it was a good day for *Taking
Risks,* so I said, "Do you know Mr. Shears?" which was like chat-
ting.

And Mrs. Alexander said, "Not really, no. I mean, I knew
him well enough to say hello and talk to a little in the street, but
I didn't know much about him. I think he worked in a bank. The
National Westminster. In town."

And I said, "Father says that he is an evil man. Do you
know why he said that? Is Mr. Shears an evil man?"

And Mrs. Alexander said, "Why are you asking me about
Mr. Shears, Christopher?"

I didn't say anything because I didn't want to be investigating Wellington's murder and that was the reason I was asking
about Mr. Shears.

But Mrs. Alexander said, "Is this about Wellington?"

And I nodded because that didn't count as being a detective.

Mrs. Alexander didn't say anything. She walked to the little red box on a pole next to the gate to the park and she put
Ivor's poo into the box, which was a brown thing inside a red
thing, which made my head feel funny so I didn't look. Then she
walked back to me.

She sucked in a big breath and said, "Perhaps it would be
best not to talk about these things, Christopher."

And I asked, "Why not?"

And she said, "Because." Then she stopped and decided to
start saying a different sentence. "Because maybe your father is
right and you shouldn't go around asking questions about this."

And I asked, "Why?"

And she said, "Because obviously he is going to find it quite
upsetting."

And I said, "Why is he going to find it upsetting?"

Then she sucked in another big breath and said, "Because . . . because I think you know why your father doesn't like Mr. Shears very much."

Then I asked, "Did Mr. Shears kill Mother?"

And Mrs. Alexander said, "Kill her?"

And I said, "Yes. Did he kill Mother?"

And Mrs. Alexander said, "No. No. Of course he didn't kill your mother."

And I said, "But did he give her stress so that she died of a heart attack?"

And Mrs. Alexander said, "I honestly don't know what you're talking about, Christopher."

And I said, "Or did he hurt her so that she had to go into hospital?"

And Mrs. Alexander said, "Did she have to go into hospital?"

And I said, "Yes. And it wasn't very serious at first, but she had a heart attack when she was in hospital."

And Mrs. Alexander said, "Oh my goodness."

I said, "And she died."

And Mrs. Alexander said "Oh my goodness" again, and then she said, "Oh, Christopher, I am so, so sorry. I never realized."

Then I asked her, "Why did you say 'I think you know why your father doesn't like Mr. Shears very much'?"

Mrs. Alexander put her hand over her mouth and said, "Oh dear, dear, dear." But she didn't answer my question.

So I asked her the same question again, because in a murder mystery novel when someone doesn't want to answer a question it is because they are trying to keep a secret or trying to stop someone from getting into trouble, which means that the answers to those questions are the most important answers of all, and that is why the detective has to put that person under pressure.

But Mrs. Alexander still didn't answer. Instead she asked me a question. She said, "So you don't know?"

And I said, "Don't know what?"

She replied, "Christopher, look, I probably shouldn't be telling you this." Then she said, "Perhaps we should take a little walk in the park together. This is not the place to be talking about this kind of thing."

I was nervous. I did not know Mrs. Alexander. I knew that she was an old lady and that she liked dogs. But she was a stranger. And I never go into the park on my own because it is dangerous and people inject drugs behind the public toilets in the corner. I wanted to go home and go up to my room and feed Toby and practice some maths.

But I was excited, too. Because I thought she might tell me a secret. And the secret might be about who killed Wellington. Or about Mr. Shears. And if she did that I might have more evidence against him, or be able to *Exclude Him from My Investiations.*

So because it was a **Super Good Day** I decided to walk into the park with Mrs. Alexander, even though it scared me.

When we were inside the park Mrs. Alexander stopped walking and said, "I am going to say something to you and you must promise not to tell your father that I told you this."

I asked, "Why?"

And she said, "I shouldn't have said what I said. And if I don't explain, you'll carry on wondering what I meant. And you might ask your father. And I don't want you to do that because I don't want you to upset him. So I'm going to explain why I said what I said. But before I do that you have to promise not to tell anyone I said this to you."

I asked, "Why?"

And she said, "Christopher, please, just trust me."

And I said, "I promise." Because if Mrs. Alexander told me who killed Wellington, or she told me that Mr. Shears had really killed Mother, I could still go to the police and tell them because you are allowed to break a promise if someone has committed a crime and you know about it.

And Mrs. Alexander said, "Your mother, before she died, was very good friends with Mr. Shears."

And I said, "I know."

And she said, "No, Christopher. I'm not sure that you do. I mean that they were very good friends. Very, very good friends."

I thought about this for a while and said, "Do you mean that they were doing sex?"

And Mrs. Alexander said, "Yes, Christopher. That is what I mean."

Then she didn't say anything for about 30 seconds.

Then she said, "I'm sorry, Christopher. I really didn't mean to say anything that was going to upset you. But I wanted to explain. Why I said what I said. You see, I thought you knew. That's why your father thinks that Mr. Shears is an evil man. And that will be why he doesn't want you going around talking to people about Mr. Shears. Because that will bring back bad memories."

And I said, "Was that why Mr. Shears left Mrs. Shears, because he was doing sex with someone else when he was married to Mrs. Shears?"

And Mrs. Alexander said, "Yes, I expect so."

Then she said, "I'm sorry, Christopher. I really am."

And I said, "I think I should go now."

And she said, "Are you OK, Christopher?"

And I said, "I'm scared of being in the park with you because you're a stranger."

And she said, "I'm not a stranger, Christopher, I'm a friend."

And I said, "I'm going to go home now."

And she said, "If you want to talk about this you can come and see me anytime you want. You only have to knock on my door."

And I said, "OK."

And she said, "Christopher?"

And I said, "What?"

And she said, "You won't tell your father about this conversation, will you?"

And I said, "No. I promised."

And she said, "You go on home. And remember what I said. Anytime."

Then I went home.

101. Mr. Jeavons said that I liked maths because it was safe. He said I liked maths because it meant solving problems, and these problems were difficult and interesting but there was always a straightforward answer at the end. And what he meant was that maths wasn't like life because in life there are no straightforward answers at the end. I know he meant this because this is what he said.

This is because Mr. Jeavons doesn't understand numbers.

Here is a famous story called **The Monty Hall Problem** which I have included in this book because it illustrates what I mean.

There used to be a column called *Ask Marilyn* in a magazine called *Parade* in America. And this column was written by Marilyn vos Savant and in the magazine it said that she had the highest IQ in the world in the *Guinness Book of World Records Hall of Fame.* And in the column she answered maths questions sent in by readers. And in September 1990 this question was sent in by Craig F. Whitaker of Columbia, Maryland (but it is not what is called a direct quote because I have made it simpler and easier to understand)

> *You are on a game show on television. On this game show the idea is to win a car as a prize. The game show host shows you three doors. He says that there is a car behind one of the doors and there are goats behind the other two doors. He asks you to pick a door. You pick a door but the door is not opened. Then the game show host opens one of the doors you didn't pick to show a goat (because he knows what is behind the doors). Then he says that you have one final chance to change your mind before the doors are opened and you get a car or a goat. So he asks you if you want to change your mind and pick the other unopened door instead. What should you do?*

Marilyn vos Savant said that you should always change and pick the final door because the chances are 2 in 3 that there will be a car behind that door.

But if you use your intuition you think that chance is 50-50 because you think there is an equal chance that the car is behind any door.

Lots of people wrote to the magazine to say that Marilyn vos Savant was wrong, even when she explained very carefully why she was right. Of the letters she got about the problem, 92% said that she was wrong and lots of these were from mathematicians and scientists. Here are some of the things that they said

> *I'm very concerned with the general public's lack of mathematical skills. Please help by confessing your error.*
>
> **Robert Sachs, Ph.D., George Mason University**

> *There is enough mathematical illiteracy in this country, and we don't need the world's highest IQ propagating more. Shame!*
>
> **Scott Smith, Ph.D., University of Florida**

> *I am in shock that after being corrected by at least three mathematicians, you still do not see your mistake.*
>
> **Kent Ford, Dickinson State University**

> *I am sure you will receive many letters from high school and college students. Perhaps you should keep a few addresses for help with future columns.*
>
> **W. Robert Smith, Ph.D., Georgia State University**

*You are utterly incorrect... How many irate
mathematicians are needed to get you to change your
mind?*

E. Ray Bobo, Ph.D., Georgetown University

*If all those Ph.D.'s were wrong, the country would be
in very serious trouble.*

Everett Harman, Ph.D., U.S. Army Research Institute

But Marilyn vos Savant was right. And here are 2 ways you can
show this.

Firstly you can do it by maths like this

Let the doors be called X, Y and Z.

Let C_x be the event that the car is behind door X and
so on.

Let H_x be the event that the host opens door X and
so on.

Supposing that you choose door X, the possibility
that you win a car if you then switch your choice is
given by the following formula

$$P(H_Z \wedge C_Y) + P(H_Y \wedge C_Z)$$

$$= P(C_Y) \cdot P(H_Z \mid C_Y) + P(C_Z) \cdot P(H_Y \mid C_Z)$$

$$= (\tfrac{1}{3} \cdot 1) + (\tfrac{1}{3} \cdot 1) = \tfrac{2}{3}$$

The second way you can work it out is by making a picture of all
the possible outcomes like this

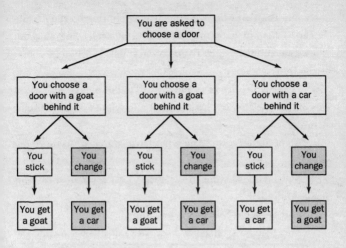

So if you change, 2 times out of 3 you get a car. And if you stick, you only get a car 1 time out of 3.

And this shows that intuition can sometimes get things wrong. And intuition is what people use in life to make decisions. But logic can help you work out the right answer.

It also shows that Mr. Jeavons was wrong and numbers are sometimes very complicated and not very straightforward at all. And that is why I like **The Monty Hall Problem.**

1 0 3.   When I got home Rhodri was there. Rhodri is the man who works for Father, helping him do heating maintenance and boiler repair. And he sometimes comes round to the house in the evening to drink beer with Father and watch the television and have a conversation.

Rhodri was wearing a pair of white dungarees which had

dirty marks all over them and he had a gold ring on the middle finger of his left hand and he smelled of something I do not know the name of which Father often smells of when he comes home from work.

I put my licorice laces and my Milky Bar in my special food box on the shelf, which Father is not allowed to touch because it is mine.

Then Father said, "And what have you been up to, young man?"

And I said, "I went to the shop to get some licorice laces and a Milky Bar."

And he said, "You were a long time."

And I said, "I talked to Mrs. Alexander's dog outside the shop. And I stroked him and he sniffed my trousers." Which was another white lie.

Then Rhodri said to me, "God, you do get the third degree, don't you."

But I didn't know what *the third degree* was.

And he said, "So, how are you doing, captain?"

And I said, "I'm doing very well, thank you," which is what you're meant to say.

And he said, "What's 251 times 864?"

And I thought about this and I said, "216,864." Because it was a really easy sum because you just multiply $864 \times 1,000$, which is **864,000.** Then you divide it by **4,** which is **216,000,** and that's 250×864. Then you just add another **864** onto it to get 251×864. And that's **216,864.**

And I said, "Is that right?"

And Rhodri said, "I haven't got a bloody clue," and he laughed.

I don't like it when Rhodri laughs at me. Rhodri laughs at me a lot. Father says it is being friendly.

Then Father said, "I'll stick one of those Gobi Aloo Sag things in the oven for you, OK?"

This is because I like Indian food because it has a strong taste. But Gobi Aloo Sag is yellow, so I put red food coloring into it before I eat it. And I keep a little plastic bottle of this in my special food box.

And I said, "OK."

And Rhodri said, "So, it looks like Parky stitched them up, then?" But this was to Father, not to me.

And Father said, "Well, those circuit boards looked like they'd come out of the bloody ark."

And Rhodri said, "You going to tell them?"

And Father said, "What's the point? They're hardly going to take him to court, are they?"

And Rhodri said, "That'll be the day."

And Father said, "Best to let sleeping dogs lie, I reckon."

Then I went into the garden.

Siobhan said that when you are writing a book you have to include some descriptions of things. I said that I could take photographs and put them in the book. But she said the idea of a book was to describe things using words so that people could read them and make a picture in their own head.

And she said it was best to describe things that were interesting or different.

She also said that I should describe people in the story by mentioning one or two details about them so that people could make a picture of them in their head. Which is why I wrote about Mr. Jeavons's shoes with all the holes in them and the policeman who looked as if he had two mice in his nose and the thing Rhodri smelled of but I didn't know the name for.

So I decided to do a description of the garden. But the garden wasn't very interesting or different. It was just a garden, with grass and a shed and a clothesline. But the sky was interesting and different because usually skies look boring because they are all blue or all gray or all covered in one pattern of clouds and they don't look like they are hundreds of miles above your head. They look like someone might have painted them on a big roof. But this sky had lots of different types of clouds in it at different heights, so you could see how big it was and this made it look enormous.

Furthest away in the sky were lots of little white clouds which looked like fish scales or sand dunes which had a very regular pattern.

Then next furthest away and to the west were some big clouds which were colored slightly orange because it was nearly evening and the sun was going down.

Then closest to the ground was a huge cloud which was colored gray because it was a rain cloud. And it was a big pointy shape and it looked like this

And when I looked at it for a long time I could see it moving very slowly and it was like an alien spaceship hundreds of kilometers long, like in *Dune* or *Blake's 7* or *Close Encounters*

of the Third Kind, except that it wasn't made of solid material, it was made of droplets of condensed water vapor, which is what clouds are made of.

And it could have been an alien spaceship.

People think that alien spaceships would be solid and made of metal and have lights all over them and move slowly through the sky because that is how we would build a spaceship if we were able to build one that big. But aliens, if they exist, would probably be very different from us. They might look like big slugs, or be flat like reflections. Or they might be bigger than planets. Or they might not have bodies at all. They might just be information, like in a computer. And their spaceships might look like clouds, or be made up of unconnected objects like dust or leaves.

Then I listened to the sounds in the garden and I could hear a bird singing and I could hear traffic noise which was like the surf on a beach and I could hear someone playing music somewhere and children shouting. And in between these noises, if I listened very carefully and stood completely still, I could hear a tiny whining noise inside my ears and the air going in and out of my nose.

Then I sniffed the air to see if I could see what the air in the garden smelled like. But I couldn't smell anything. It smelled of nothing. And this was interesting, too.

Then I went inside and fed Toby.

1 0 7 .   *The Hound of the Baskervilles* is my favorite book.

In *The Hound of the Baskervilles,* Sherlock Holmes and Doctor Watson get a visit from James Mortimer, who is a doctor from the moors in Devon. James Mortimer's friend, Sir Charles Baskerville, has died of a heart attack and James Mortimer thinks that he might have been scared to death. James Mortimer also has an ancient scroll which describes the curse of the Baskervilles.

On this scroll it says that Sir Charles Baskerville had an ancestor called Sir Hugo Baskerville, who was a wild, profane and godless man. And he tried to do sex with a daughter of a yeoman, but she escaped and he chased her across the moor. And his friends, who were daredevil roisterers, chased after him.

And when they found him, the daughter of the yeoman had died of exhaustion and fatigue. And they saw a great black beast, shaped like a hound yet larger than any hound that ever mortal eye has rested on, and this hound was tearing the throat out of Sir Hugo Baskerville. And one of the friends died of fear that very night and the other two were broken men for the rest of their days.

James Mortimer thinks that the Hound of the Baskervilles might have scared Sir Charles to death and he is worried that his son and heir, Sir Henry Baskerville, will be in danger when he goes to the hall in Devon.

So Sherlock Holmes sends Doctor Watson to Devon with Sir Henry Baskerville and James Mortimer. And Doctor Watson tries to work out who might have killed Sir Charles Baskerville. And Sherlock Holmes says he will stay in London, but he travels to Devon secretly and does investigations of his own.

And Sherlock Holmes finds out that Sir Charles was killed by a neighbor called Stapleton who is a butterfly collector and a distant relation of the Baskervilles. And Stapleton is poor, so he tries to kill Sir Henry Baskerville so that he will inherit the hall.

In order to do this he has brought a huge dog from London

and covered it in phosphorus to make it glow in the dark, and it was this dog which scared Sir Charles Baskerville to death. And Sherlock Holmes and Watson and Lestrade from Scotland Yard catch him. And Sherlock Holmes and Watson shoot the dog, which is one of the dogs which gets killed in the story, which is not nice because it is not the dog's fault. And Stapleton escapes into the Grimpen Mire, which is part of the moor, and he dies because he is sucked into a bog.

There are some bits of the story I don't like. One bit is the ancient scroll because it is written in old language which is difficult to understand, like this

> *Learn then from this story not to fear the fruits of the past, but rather to be circumspect in the future, that those foul passions whereby our family has suffered so grievously may not again be loosed to our undoing.*

And sometimes Sir Arthur Conan Doyle (who is the author) describes people like this

> *There was something subtly wrong with the face, some coarseness of expression, some hardness, perhaps of eye, some looseness of lip which marred its perfect beauty.*

And I don't know what *some hardness, perhaps of eye* means, and I'm not interested in faces.

But sometimes it is fun not knowing what the words mean because you can look them up in a dictionary, like *goyal* (which is a deep dip) or *tors* (which are hills or rocky heights).

I like **The Hound of the Baskervilles** because it is a detective story, which means that there are clues and Red Herrings.

These are some of the clues

1. Two of Sir Henry Baskerville's boots go missing when he is staying at a hotel in London. This means that someone wants to give them to the Hound of the Baskervilles to smell, like a bloodhound, so that it can chase him. This means that the Hound of the Baskervilles is not a supernatural being but a real dog.

2. Stapleton is the only person who knows how to get through the Grimpen Mire and he tells Watson to stay out of it for his own safety. This means that he is hiding something in the middle of the Grimpen Mire and doesn't want anyone else to find it.

3. Mrs. Stapleton tells Doctor Watson to "go straight back to London instantly." This is because she thinks Doctor Watson is Sir Henry Baskerville and she knows that her husband wants to kill him.

And these are some of the Red Herrings

1. Sherlock Holmes and Watson are followed when they are in London by a man in a coach with a black beard. This makes you think that the man is Barrymore, who is the caretaker at Baskerville Hall, because he is the only other person who has a black beard. But the man is really Stapleton, who is wearing a false beard.

2. Selden, the Notting Hill murderer. This is a man who has escaped from a prison nearby and is being hunted down on the moors, which makes you think that he has something to do with the story, because he is a criminal, but he hasn't anything to do with the story at all.

3. The Man on the Tor. This is a silhouette of a man that Doctor Watson sees on the moor at night and doesn't recognize, which makes you think it is the murderer. But it is Sherlock Holmes who has come to Devon secretly.

I also like *The Hound of the Baskervilles* because I like Sherlock Holmes and I think that if I were a proper detective he is the kind of detective I would be. He is very intelligent and he solves the mystery and he says

The world is full of obvious things which nobody by any chance ever observes.

But he notices them, like I do. Also it says in the book

Sherlock Holmes had, in a very remarkable degree, the power of detaching his mind at will.

And this is like me, too, because if I get really interested in something, like practicing maths, or reading a book about the Apollo missions or great white sharks, I don't notice anything else and Father can be calling me to come and eat my supper and I won't hear him. And this is why I am very good at playing chess, because I detach my mind at will and concentrate on the board and after a while the person I am playing will stop concentrating and start scratching their nose, or staring out of the window, and then they will make a mistake and I will win.

Also Doctor Watson says about Sherlock Holmes

His mind... was busy in endeavouring to frame some
scheme into which all these strange and apparently
disconnected episodes could be fitted.

And that is what I am trying to do by writing this book.

Also Sherlock Holmes doesn't believe in the supernatural, which is God and fairy tales and Hounds of Hell and curses, which are stupid things.

And I am going to finish this chapter with two interesting facts about Sherlock Holmes

1. In the original Sherlock Holmes stories Sherlock Holmes is never described as wearing a deerstalker hat, which is what he is always wearing in pictures and cartoons. The deerstalker hat was invented by a man called Sidney Paget, who did the illustrations for the original books.

2. In the original Sherlock Holmes stories Sherlock Holmes never says "Elementary, my dear Watson." He only ever says this in films and on the television.

1 0 9. That night I wrote some more of my book, and the next morning I took it into school so that Siobhan could read it and tell me if I had made mistakes with the spelling and the grammar.

Siobhan read the book during morning break when she has a cup of coffee and sits at the edge of the playground with the other teachers. And after morning break she came and sat down next to me and said she had read the bit about my conversation with Mrs. Alexander and she said, "Have you told your father about this?"

And I replied, "No."

And she said, "Are you going to tell your father about this?"

And I replied, "No."

And she said, "Good. I think that's a good idea, Christopher." And then she said, "Did it make you sad to find this out?"

And I asked, "Find what out?"

And she said, "Did it make you upset to find out that your mother and Mr. Shears had an affair?"

And I said, "No."

And she said, "Are you telling the truth, Christopher?"

And then I said, "I always tell the truth."

And she said, "I know you do, Christopher. But sometimes we get sad about things and we don't like to tell other people that we are sad about them. We like to keep it a secret. Or sometimes we are sad but we don't really know we are sad. So we say we aren't sad. But really we are."

And I said, "I'm not sad."

And she said, "If you do start to feel sad about this, I want you to know that you can come and talk to me about it. Because I think talking to me will help you feel less sad. And if you don't feel sad but you just want to talk to me about it, that would be OK, too. Do you understand?"

And I said, "I understand."

And she said, "Good."

And I replied, "But I don't feel sad about it. Because Mother is dead. And because Mr. Shears isn't around anymore. So I would be feeling sad about something that isn't real and doesn't exist. And that would be stupid."

And then I practiced maths for the rest of the morning and

at lunch I didn't have the quiche because it was yellow, but I did have the carrots and the peas and lots of tomato ketchup. And for afters I had some blackberry and apple crumble, but not the crumble bit because that was yellow, too, and I got Mrs. Davis to take the crumble bit off before she put it onto my plate because it doesn't matter if different sorts of food are touching before they are actually on your plate.

Then, after lunch, I spent the afternoon doing art with Mrs. Peters and I painted some pictures of aliens which looked like this

113. My memory is like a film. That is why I am really good at remembering things, like the conversations I have written down in this book, and what people were wearing, and what they smelled like, because my memory has a smelltrack which is like a soundtrack.

And when people ask me to remember something I can simply press **Rewind** and **Fast Forward** and **Pause** like on a video recorder, but more like a DVD player because I don't have to Rewind through everything in between to get to a memory of something a long time ago. And there are no buttons, either, because it is happening in my head.

If someone says to me, "Christopher, tell me what your mother was like," I can Rewind to lots of different scenes and say what she was like in those scenes.

For example, I could Rewind to 4 July 1992 when I was 9 years old, which was a Saturday, and we were on holiday in Cornwall and in the afternoon we were on the beach in a place called Polperro. And Mother was wearing a pair of shorts made out of denim and a light blue bikini top and she was smoking cigarettes called Consulate which were mint flavor. And she wasn't swimming. Mother was sunbathing on a towel which had red and purple stripes and she was reading a book by Georgette Heyer called *The Masqueraders.* And then she finished sunbathing and went into the water to swim and she said, "Bloody Nora, it's cold." And she said I should come and swim, too, but I don't like swimming because I don't like taking my clothes off. And she said I should just roll up my trousers and walk into the water a little way, so I did. And I stood in the water. And Mother said, "Look. It's lovely." And she jumped backward and disappeared under the water and I thought a shark had eaten her and I screamed and she stood up out of the water again and came over to where I was standing and held up her right hand and spread her fingers out in a fan and said, "Come on, Christopher, touch my hand. Come on now. Stop screaming. Touch my hand. Listen to me, Christopher. You can do it." And after a while I stopped screaming and I held up my left hand and spread my fingers out in a fan and we made our fingers and thumbs touch each other and Mother said, "It's OK, Christopher. It's OK. There aren't any sharks in Cornwall," and then I felt better.

Except I can't remember anything before I was about 4 because I wasn't looking at things in the right way before then, so they didn't get recorded properly.

And this is how I recognize someone if I don't know who they are. I see what they are wearing, or if they have a walking stick, or funny hair, or a certain type of glasses, or they have a particular way of moving their arms, and I do a **Search** through my memories to see if I have met them before.

And this is also how I know how to act in difficult situations when I don't know what to do.

For example, if people say things which don't make sense, like, "See you later, alligator," or "You'll catch your death in that," I do a Search and see if I have ever heard someone say this before.

And if someone is lying on the floor at school, I do a Search through my memory to find a picture of someone having an epileptic fit and then I compare the picture with what is happening in front of me so I can decide whether they are just lying down and playing a game, or having a sleep, or whether they are having an epileptic fit. And if they are having an epileptic fit, I move any furniture out of the way to stop them from banging their head and I take my jumper off and I put it underneath their head and I go and find a teacher.

Other people have pictures in their heads, too. But they are different because the pictures in my head are all pictures of things which really happened. But other people have pictures in their heads of things which aren't real and didn't happen.

For example, sometimes Mother used to say, "If I hadn't married your father I think I'd be living in a little farmhouse in the south of France with someone called Jean. And he'd be, ooh, a local handyman. You know, doing painting and decorating for people, gardening, building fences. And we'd have a veranda with figs growing over it and there would be a field of sunflowers at the bottom of the garden and a little town on the hill in the distance and we'd sit outside in the evening and drink red wine and smoke Gauloises cigarettes and watch the sun go down."

And Siobhan once said that when she felt depressed or sad she would close her eyes and she would imagine that she was staying in a house on Cape Cod with her friend Elly, and they would take a trip on a boat from Provincetown and go out into the bay to watch the humpback whales and that made her feel calm and peaceful and happy.

And sometimes, when someone has died, like Mother died, people say, "What would you want to say to your mother if she was here now?" or "What would your mother think about that?" which is stupid because Mother is dead and you can't say anything to people who are dead and dead people can't think.

And Grandmother has pictures in her head, too, but her pictures are all confused, like someone has muddled the film up and she can't tell what happened in what order, so she thinks that dead people are still alive and she doesn't know whether something happened in real life or whether it happened on television.

127. When I got home from school Father was still out at work, so I unlocked the front door and went inside and took my coat off. I went into the kitchen and put my things on the table. And one of the things was this book which I had taken into school to show to Siobhan. I made myself a raspberry milk shake and heated it up in the microwave and then went through to the living room to watch one of my *Blue Planet* videos about life in the deepest parts of the ocean.

The video was about the sea creatures who live around sulfur chimneys, which are underwater volcanoes where gases are ejected from the earth's crust into the water. Scientists never expected there to be any living organisms there because it was so hot and so poisonous, but there are whole ecosystems there.

I like this bit because it shows you that there is always something new that science can discover, and all the facts that you take for granted can be completely wrong. And also I like the fact that they are filming in a place which is harder to get to than the top of Mount Everest but is only a few miles away from sea level. And it is one of the quietest and darkest and most secret places on the surface of the earth. And I like imagining that I am there sometimes, in a spherical metal submersible with windows that are 30 cm thick to stop them from imploding under the pressure. And I imagine that I am the only person inside it, and that it is not connected to a ship at all but can operate under its own power and I can control the motors and move anywhere I want to on the seabed and I can never be found.

Father came home at 5:48 p.m. I heard him come through the front door. Then he came into the living room. He was wearing a lime green and sky blue check shirt and there was a double knot on one of his shoes but not on the other. He was carrying an old advert for Fussell's Milk Powder which was made of metal and painted with blue and white enamel and covered with little circles of rust which were like bullet holes, but he didn't explain why he was carrying this.

He said, "Howdy, pardner," which is a joke he does.

And I said, "Hello."

I carried on watching the video and Father went into the kitchen.

I had forgotten that I had left my book lying on the kitchen table because I was too interested in the *Blue Planet* video. This is what is called *Relaxing Your Guard*, and it is what you must never do if you are a detective.

It was 5:54 p.m. when Father came back into the living room. He said, "What is this?" but he said it very quietly and I didn't realize that he was angry because he wasn't shouting.

He was holding the book in his right hand.

I said, "It's a book I'm writing."

And he said, "Is this true? Did you talk to Mrs. Alexander?" He said this very quietly as well, so I still didn't realize that he was angry.

And I said, "Yes."

Then he said, "Holy fucking Jesus, Christopher. How stupid are you?"

This is what Siobhan says is called a rhetorical question. It has a question mark at the end, but you are not meant to answer it because the person who is asking it already knows the answer. It is difficult to spot a rhetorical question.

Then Father said, "What the fuck did I tell you, Christopher?" This was much louder.

And I replied, "Not to mention Mr. Shears's name in our house. And not to go asking Mrs. Shears, or anyone, about who killed that bloody dog. And not to go trespassing in other people's gardens. And to stop this ridiculous bloody detective game. Except I haven't done any of those things. I just asked Mrs. Alexander about Mr. Shears because——"

But Father interrupted me and said, "Don't give me that bollocks, you little shit. You knew exactly what you were bloody doing. I've read the book, remember." And when he said this he held up the book and shook it. "What else did I say, Christopher?"

I thought that this might be another rhetorical question,

but I wasn't sure. I found it hard to work out what to say because I was starting to get scared and confused.

Then Father repeated the question, "What else did I say, Christopher?"

I said, "I don't know."

And he said, "Come on. You're the fucking memory man."

But I couldn't think.

And Father said, "Not to go around sticking your fucking nose into other people's business. And what do you do? You go around sticking your nose into other people's business. You go around raking up the past and sharing it with every Tom, Dick and Harry you bump into. What am I going to do with you, Christopher? What the fuck am I going to do with you?"

I said, "I was just doing chatting with Mrs. Alexander. I wasn't doing investigating."

And he said, "I ask you to do one thing for me, Christopher. One thing."

And I said, "I didn't want to talk to Mrs. Alexander. It was Mrs. Alexander who—"

But Father interrupted me and grabbed hold of my arm really hard.

Father had never grabbed hold of me like that before. Mother had hit me sometimes because she was a very hot-tempered person, which means that she got angry more quickly than other people and she shouted more often. But Father was a more levelheaded person, which means he didn't get angry as quickly and he didn't shout as often. So I was very surprised when he grabbed me.

I don't like it when people grab me. And I don't like being surprised either. So I hit him, like I hit the policeman when he took hold of my arms and lifted me onto my feet. But Father didn't let go, and he was shouting. And I hit him again. And then I didn't know what I was doing anymore.

I had no memories for a short while. I know it was a short while because I checked my watch afterward. It was like someone had switched me off and then switched me on again. And when they switched me on again I was sitting on the carpet with my back against the wall and there was blood on my right hand and the side of my head was hurting. And Father was standing on the carpet a meter in front of me looking down at me and he was still holding my book in his right hand, but it was bent in half and all the corners were messed up, and there was a scratch on his neck and a big rip in the sleeve of his green and blue check shirt and he was breathing really deeply.

After about a minute he turned and walked through to the kitchen. Then he unlocked the back door into the garden and went outside. I heard him lift the lid of the dustbin and drop something into it and put the lid of the dustbin back on. Then he came into the kitchen again, but he wasn't carrying the book anymore. Then he locked the back door again and put the key into the little china jug that is shaped like a fat nun and he stood in the middle of the kitchen and closed his eyes.

Then he opened his eyes and he said, "I need a fucking drink."

And he got himself a can of beer.

131. These are some of the reasons why I hate yellow and brown

YELLOW

    1. Custard

    2. Bananas (bananas also turn brown)

    3. Double Yellow Lines

    4. Yellow Fever (which is a disease from tropical America and West Africa which causes a high fever, acute nephritis, jaundice and hemorrhages, and it is caused by a virus transmitted by the bite of a mosquito called *Aëdes aegypti*, which used to be called *Stegomyia fasciata*; and nephritis is inflammation of the kidneys)

    5. Yellow Flowers (because I get hay fever from flower pollen, which is one of 3 sorts of hay fever, and the others are from grass pollen and fungus pollen, and it makes me feel ill)

    6. Sweet Corn (because it comes out in your poo and you don't digest it so you are not really meant to eat it, like grass or leaves)

BROWN

    1. Dirt

    2. Gravy

    3. Poo

    4. Wood (because people used to make machines and vehicles out of wood, but they don't anymore because wood breaks and goes rotten and has worms in it sometimes, and now people make machines and vehicles out of metal and plastic, which are much better and more modern)

    5. Melissa Brown (who is a girl at school, who is

not actually brown like Anil or Mohammed, it's just her name, but she tore my big astronaut painting into two pieces and I threw it away even after Mrs. Peters sellotaped it together again because it looked broken)

Mrs. Forbes said that hating yellow and brown is just being silly. And Siobhan said that she shouldn't say things like that and everyone has favorite colors. And Siobhan was right. But Mrs. Forbes was a bit right, too. Because it is sort of being silly. But in life you have to take lots of decisions and if you don't take decisions you would never do anything because you would spend all your time choosing between things you could do. So it is good to have a reason why you hate some things and you like others. It is like being in a restaurant like when Father takes me out to a Berni Inn sometimes and you look at the menu and you have to choose what you are going to have. But you don't know if you are going to like something because you haven't tasted it yet, so you have favorite foods and you choose these, and you have foods you don't like and you don't choose these, and then it is simple.

137. The next day Father said he was sorry that he had hit me and he didn't mean to. He made me wash the cut on my cheek with Dettol to make sure that it wasn't infected, then he got me to put a plaster on it so it didn't bleed.

Then, because it was Saturday, he said he was going to take me on an expedition to show me that he was properly sorry, and we were going to Twycross Zoo. So he made me some sandwiches with white bread and tomatoes and lettuce and ham and strawberry jam for me to eat because I don't like eating food from places I don't know. And he said it would be OK because there wouldn't be too many people at the zoo because it was forecast to rain, and I was glad about that because I don't like crowds of people and I like it when it is raining. So I went and got my waterproof, which is orange.

Then we drove to Twycross Zoo.

I had never been to Twycross Zoo before so I didn't have a route worked out in my mind before we got there, so we bought a guidebook from the information center and then we walked round the whole zoo and I decided which were my favorite animals.

My favorite animals were

1. **RANDYMAN,** which is the name of the oldest **Red-Faced Black Spider Monkey** *(Ateles paniscus paniscus)* ever kept in captivity. Randyman is 44 years old, which is the same age as Father. He used to be a pet on a ship and have a metal band round his stomach, like in a story about pirates.

2. The **PATAGONIAN SEA LIONS,** which are called **Miracle** and **Star.**

3. **MALIKU,** which is an **Orangutan.** I liked it especially because it was lying in a kind of hammock made out of a pair of stripy green pajama bottoms and on the blue plastic notice next to the cage it said it made the hammock itself.

Then we went to the café and Father had plaice and chips and apple pie and ice cream and a pot of Earl Grey tea and I had my sandwiches and I read the guidebook to the zoo.

And Father said, "I love you very much, Christopher. Don't ever forget that. And I know I lose my rag occasionally. I know I get angry. I know I shout. And I know I shouldn't. But I only do it because I worry about you, because I don't want to see you getting into trouble, because I don't want you to get hurt. Do you understand?"

I didn't know whether I understood. So I said, "I don't know."

And Father said, "Christopher, do you understand that I love you?"

And I said "Yes," because loving someone is helping them when they get into trouble, and looking after them, and telling them the truth, and Father looks after me when I get into trouble, like coming to the police station, and he looks after me by cooking meals for me, and he always tells me the truth, which means that he loves me.

And then he held up his right hand and spread his fingers out in a fan, and I held up my left hand and spread my fingers out in a fan and we made our fingers and thumbs touch each other.

Then I got out a piece of paper from my bag and I did a map of the zoo from memory as a test. The map was like this

[10] The dhole is *the Indian wild dog* and it looks like a fox.

[11] The langur is *the entellus monkey*.

Then we went and looked at the giraffes. And the smell of their poo was like the smell inside the gerbil cage at school when we had gerbils, and when they ran their legs were so long it looked like they were running in slow motion.

Then Father said we had to get home before the roads got busy.

139.   I like Sherlock Holmes, but I do not like Sir Arthur Conan Doyle, who was the author of the Sherlock Holmes stories. That is because he wasn't like Sherlock Holmes and he believed in the supernatural. And when he got old he joined the Spiritualist Society, which meant that he believed you could communicate with the dead. This was because his son died of influenza during the First World War and he still wanted to talk to him.

And in 1917 something famous happened called **The Case of the Cottingley Fairies.** Two cousins called Frances Griffiths, who was 9 years old, and Elsie Wright, who was 16 years old, said they used to play with fairies by a stream called Cottingley Beck and they used Frances's father's camera to take 5 photographs of the fairies like this

But they weren't real fairies. They were drawings on pieces of paper that they cut out and stood up with pins, because Elsie was a really good artist.

Harold Snelling, who was an expert in fake photography, said

> These dancing figures are not made of paper nor any fabric; they are not painted on a photographic background—but what gets me most is that all these figures have moved during the exposure.

But he was being stupid because paper would move during an exposure, and the exposure was very long because in the photograph you can see a little waterfall in the background and it is blurred.

Then Sir Arthur Conan Doyle heard about the pictures and he said he believed they were real in an article in a magazine called *The Strand.* But he was being stupid, too, because if you look at the pictures you can see that the fairies look just like fairies in old books and they have wings and dresses and tights and shoes, which is like aliens landing on earth and being like Daleks from *Doctor Who* or Imperial Stormtroopers from the Death Star in *Star Wars* or little green men like in cartoons of aliens.

And in 1981 a man called Joe Cooper interviewed Elsie Wright and Frances Griffiths for an article in a magazine called *The Unexplained* and Elsie Wright said all 5 photographs had been faked and Frances Griffiths said 4 had been faked but one was real. And they said Elsie had drawn the fairies from a book called *Princess Mary's Gift Book* by Arthur Shepperson.

And this shows that sometimes people want to be stupid and they do not want to know the truth.

And it shows that something called Occam's razor is true. And Occam's razor is not a razor that men shave with but a Law, and it says

Entia non sunt multiplicanda praeter necessitatem.

Which is Latin and it means

No more things should be presumed to exist than are absolutely necessary.

Which means that a murder victim is usually killed by someone known to them and fairies are made out of paper and you can't talk to someone who is dead.

149. When I went to school on Monday, Siobhan asked me why I had a bruise on the side of my face. I said that Father was angry and he had grabbed me so I had hit him and then we had a fight. Siobhan asked whether Father had hit me and I said I didn't know because I got very cross and it made my memory go strange. And then she asked if Father had hit me because he was angry. And I said he didn't hit me, he grabbed me, but he was angry. And Siobhan asked if he grabbed me hard, and I said that he had grabbed me hard. And Siobhan asked if I was frightened about going home, and I said I wasn't. And then she asked me if I wanted to talk about it anymore, and I said that I didn't. And then she said, "OK," and we didn't talk about it anymore, because grabbing is OK if it is on your arm or your shoulder when you are angry, but you can't grab someone's hair or their face. But hitting is not allowed, except if you are already in a fight with someone, then it is not so bad.

And when I got home from school Father was still at work, so I went into the kitchen and took the key out of the little china jug shaped like a nun and opened the back door and went outside and looked inside the dustbin to find my book.

I wanted to get my book back because I liked writing it. I liked having a project to do and I liked it especially if it was a difficult project like a book. Also I still didn't know who had killed Wellington and my book was where I had kept all the clues that I had discovered and I did not want them to be thrown away.

But my book wasn't in the dustbin.

I put the lid back on the dustbin and walked down the garden to have a look in the bin where Father keeps the garden waste, such as lawn clippings and apples that have fallen off the trees, but my book wasn't in there either.

I wondered if Father had put it into his van and driven to the tip and put it into one of the big bins there, but I did not want that to be true because then I would never see it again.

One other possibility was that Father had hidden my book somewhere in the house. So I decided to do some detecting and see if I could find it. Except I had to keep listening really hard all the time so I would hear his van when he pulled up outside the house so he wouldn't catch me being a detective.

I started by looking in the kitchen. My book was approximately $25 \text{ cm} \times 35 \text{ cm} \times 1 \text{ cm}$ so it couldn't be hidden in a very small place, which meant that I didn't have to look in any really small places. I looked on top of the cupboards and down the back of drawers and under the oven and I used my special Mag-Lite torch and a piece of mirror from the utility room to help me see into the dark spaces at the back of the cupboards where the mice used to get in from the garden and have their babies.

Then I detected in the utility room.

Then I detected in the dining room.

Then I detected in the living room, where I found the missing wheel from my Airfix Messerschmitt Bf 109 G-6 model under the sofa.

Then I thought I heard Father coming through the front door and I jumped and I tried to stand up fast and I banged my knee on the corner of the coffee table and it hurt a lot, but it was only one of the drug people next door dropping something on the floor.

Then I went upstairs, but I didn't do any detecting in my own room because I reasoned that Father wouldn't hide something from me in my own room unless he was being very clever and doing what is called a *Double Bluff* like in a real murder mystery novel, so I decided to look in my own room only if I couldn't find the book anywhere else.

I detected in the bathroom, but the only place to look was in the airing cupboard and there was nothing in there.

Which meant that the only room left to detect in was Father's bedroom. I didn't know whether I should look in there because he had told me before not to mess with anything in his room. But if he was going to hide something from me, the best place to hide it would be in his room.

So I told myself I would not mess with things in his room. I would move them and then I would move them back. And he would never know I had done it so he wouldn't be angry.

I started by looking under the bed. There were 7 shoes and

a comb with lots of hair in it and a piece of copper pipe and a chocolate biscuit and a porn magazine called *Fiesta* and a dead bee and a Homer Simpson pattern tie and a wooden spoon, but not my book.

Then I looked in the drawers on either side of the dressing table, but these only contained aspirin and nail clippers and batteries and dental floss and a tampon and tissues and a spare false tooth in case Father lost the false tooth he had to fill the gap where he knocked a tooth out when he fell off the ladder putting a bird box up in the garden, but my book wasn't in there either.

Then I looked in his clothes cupboard. This was full of his clothes on hangers. There was also a little shelf at the top which I could see onto if I stood on the bed, but I had to take my shoes off in case I left a dirty footprint that would be a clue if Father decided to do some detecting. But the only things on the shelf were more porn magazines and a broken sandwich toaster and 12 wire coat hangers and an old hair dryer that used to belong to Mother.

In the bottom of the cupboard was a large plastic toolbox which was full of tools for doing Do It Yourself, like a drill and a paintbrush and some screws and a hammer, but I could see these without opening the box because it was made of transparent gray plastic.

Then I saw that there was another box underneath the toolbox, so I lifted the toolbox out of the cupboard. The other box was an old cardboard box that is called a shirt box because people used to buy shirts in them. And when I opened the shirt box I saw my book was inside it.

Then I didn't know what to do.

I was happy because Father hadn't thrown my book away. But if I took the book he would know I had been messing with things in his room and he would be very angry and I had promised not to mess with things in his room.

Then I heard his van pulling up outside the house and I knew that I had to think fast and be clever. So I decided that I would leave the book where it was because I reasoned that Father wasn't going to throw it away if he had put it into the shirt box and I could carry on writing in another book that I would keep really secret and then, maybe later, he might change his mind and let me have the first book back again and I could copy the new book into it. And if he never gave it back to me I would be able to remember most of what I had written, so I would put it all into the second secret book and if there were bits I wanted to check to make sure I had remembered them correctly I could come into his room when he was out and check.

Then I heard Father shutting the door of the van.

And that was when I saw the envelope.

It was an envelope addressed to me and it was lying under my book in the shirt box with some other envelopes. I picked it up. It had never been opened. It said

Christopher Boone
36 Randolph Street
Swindon
Wiltshire

Then I noticed that there were lots of other envelopes and they were all addressed to me. And this was interesting and confusing.

And then I noticed how the words Christopher and Swindon were written. They were written like this

Christopher
Swinden

I only know 3 people who do little circles instead of dots over the letter *i*. And one of them is Siobhan, and one of them was Mr. Loxely, who used to teach at the school, and one of them was Mother.

And then I heard Father opening the front door, so I took one envelope from under the book and I put the lid back on the shirt box and I put the toolbox back on top of it and I closed the cupboard door really carefully.

Then Father called out, "Christopher?"

I said nothing because he might be able to hear where I was calling from. I stood up and walked around the bed to the door, holding the envelope, trying to make as little noise as possible.

Father was standing at the bottom of the stairs and I thought he might see me, but he was flicking through the post which had come that morning so his head was pointing downward. Then he walked away from the foot of the stairs toward the kitchen and I closed the door of his room very quietly and went into my own room.

I wanted to look at the envelope but I didn't want to make Father angry, so I hid the envelope underneath my mattress. Then I walked downstairs and said hello to Father.

And he said, "So, what have you been up to today, young man?"

And I said, "Today we did *Life Skills* with Mrs. Gray. Which was *Using Money* and *Public Transport*. And I had tomato soup for lunch, and 3 apples. And I practiced some maths in the afternoon and we went for a walk in the park with Mrs. Peters and collected leaves for making collages."

And Father said, "Excellent, excellent. What do you fancy for chow tonight?"

Chow is food.

I said I wanted baked beans and broccoli.

And Father said, "I think that can be very easily arranged."

Then I sat on the sofa and I read some more of the book I was reading called *Chaos* by James Gleick.

Then I went into the kitchen and had my baked beans and broccoli while Father had sausages and eggs and fried bread and a mug of tea.

Then Father said, "I'm going to put those shelves up in the living room, if that's all right with you. I'll make a bit of a racket, I'm afraid, so if you want to watch television we're going to have to shift it upstairs."

And I said, "I'll go and be on my own in my room."

And he said, "Good man."

And I said, "Thank you for supper," because that is being polite.

And he said, "No problem, kiddo."

And I went up to my room.

And when I was in my room I shut the door and I took out the envelope from underneath my mattress. I held the letter up to the light to see if I could detect what was inside the envelope, but the paper of the envelope was too thick. I wondered whether I should open the envelope because it was something I had taken from Father's room. But then I reasoned that it was addressed to me so it belonged to me so it was OK to open it.

So I opened the envelope.

Inside there was a letter.

And this was what was written in the letter

451c Chapter Road
Willesden
London NW2 5NG
0208 887 8907

Dear Christopher,

I'm sorry it's been such a very long time since I wrote my last letter to you. I've been very busy. I've got a new job working as a secretery for a factory that makes things out of steel. You'd like it a lot. The factory is full of huge machines that make the steel and cut it and bend it into watever shapes they need. This week they're making a roof for a cafe in a shopping centre in Birmingham. It's shaped like a huge flower and they're going to stretch canvas over it to make it look like an enormus tent.

Also we've moved into the new flat at last as you can see from the address. It's not as nice as the old one and I don't like Willesden very much, but it's easier for Roger to get to work and he's bought it (he only rented the other one), so we can get our own furnature and paint the walls the colour we want to.

And that's why it's such a long time since I wrote my last letter to you because it's been hard work packing up all our things and then unpacking them and then getting used to this new job.

I'm very tired now and I must go to sleep and I want to put this into the letterbox tomorrow morning, so I'll sign off now and write you another letter soon.

You haven't written to me yet, so I know that you are proba-

bly still angry with me. I'm sorry Christopher. But I still love you. I hope you don't stay angry with me forever. And I'd love it if you were able to write me a letter (but remember to send it to the new address!).

I think about you all the time.

Lots of Love,
Your Mum
X X X X X

Then I was really confused because Mother had never worked as a secretary for a firm that made things out of steel. Mother had worked as a secretary for a big garage in the center of town. And Mother had never lived in London. Mother had always lived with us. And Mother had never written a letter to me before.

There was no date on the letter so I couldn't work out when Mother had written the letter and I wondered whether someone else had written the letter and pretended to be Mother.

And then I looked at the front of the envelope and I saw that there was a postmark and there was a date on the postmark and it was quite difficult to read, but it said

Which meant that the letter was posted on 16 October 1997, which was 18 months after Mother had died.

And then the door of my bedroom opened and Father said, "What are you doing?"

I said, "I'm reading a letter."

And he said, "I've finished the drilling. That David Attenborough nature program's on telly if you're interested."

I said, "OK."

Then he went downstairs again.

I looked at the letter and thought really hard. It was a mystery and I couldn't work it out. Perhaps the letter was in the wrong envelope and it had been written before Mother had died. But why was she writing from London? The longest she had been away was a week when she went to visit her cousin Ruth, who had cancer, but Ruth lived in Manchester.

And then I thought that perhaps it wasn't a letter from Mother. Perhaps it was a letter to another person called Christopher, from that Christopher's mother.

I was excited. When I started writing my book there was only one mystery I had to solve. Now there were two.

I decided that I would not think about it anymore that night because I didn't have enough information and could easily *Leap to the Wrong Conclusions* like Mr. Athelney Jones of Scotland Yard, which is a dangerous thing to do because you should make sure you have all the available clues before you start deducing things. That way you are much less likely to make a mistake.

I decided that I would wait until Father was out of the house. Then I would go into the cupboard in his bedroom and look at the other letters and see who they were from and what they said.

I folded the letter and hid it under my mattress in case Father found it and got cross. Then I went downstairs and watched the television.

151.   Lots of things are mysteries. But that doesn't mean there isn't an answer to them. It's just that scientists haven't found the answer yet.

For example, some people believe in the ghosts of people who have come back from the dead. And Uncle Terry said that he saw a ghost in a shoe shop in a shopping center in Northampton because he was going down into the basement when he saw someone dressed in gray walk across the bottom of the stairs. But when he got to the bottom of the stairs the basement was empty and there were no doors.

When he told the lady on the till upstairs, they said it was called Tuck and he was a ghost of a Franciscan friar who used to live in the monastery which was on the same site hundreds of years ago, which was why the shopping center was called **Greyfriars Shopping Center,** and they were used to him and not frightened at all.

Eventually scientists will discover something that explains ghosts, just like they discovered electricity, which explained lightning, and it might be something about people's brains, or something about the earth's magnetic field, or it might be some new force altogether. And then ghosts won't be mysteries. They will be like electricity and rainbows and nonstick frying pans.

But sometimes a mystery isn't a mystery. And this is an example of a mystery which isn't a mystery.

We have a pond at the school, with frogs in it, which are there so we can learn how to treat animals with kindness and respect, because some of the children at school are horrible to animals and think it's funny to crush worms or throw stones at cats.

And some years there are lots of frogs in the pond, and

some years there are very few. And if you drew a graph of how many frogs there were in the pond, it would look like this (but this graph is what's called *hypothetical*, which means that the numbers aren't the real numbers, it is just an *illustration*)

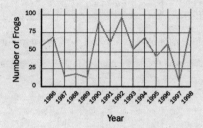

And if you looked at the graph you might think that there was a really cold winter in 1987 and 1988 and 1989 and 1997, or that there was a heron which came and ate lots of the frogs (sometimes there is a heron who comes and tries to eat the frogs, but there is chicken wire over the pond to stop it).

But sometimes it has nothing to do with cold winters or cats or herons. Sometimes it is just maths.

Here is a formula for a population of animals

$$N_{new} = \lambda \, (N_{old}) \, (1 - N_{old})$$

And in this formula N stands for the population density. When $N = 1$ the population is the biggest it can get. And when $N = 0$ the population is extinct. N_{new} is the population in one year, and N_{old} is the population in the year before. And λ is what is called a constant.

When λ is less than 1, the population gets smaller and smaller and goes extinct. And when λ is between 1 and 3, the population gets bigger and then it stays stable like this (and these graphs are hypothetical, too)

And when λ is between 3 and 3.57 the population goes in cycles like this

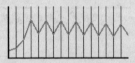

But when λ is greater than 3.57 the population becomes chaotic like in the first graph.

This was discovered by Robert May and George Oster and Jim Yorke. And it means that sometimes things are so complicated that it is impossible to predict what they are going to do next, but they are only obeying really simple rules.

And it means that sometimes a whole population of frogs, or worms, or people, can die for no reason whatsoever, just because that is the way the numbers work.

157. It was six days before I could go back into Father's room to look in the shirt box in the cupboard.

On the first day, which was a Wednesday, Joseph Fleming took his trousers off and went to the toilet all over the floor of the changing room and started to eat it, but Mr. Davis stopped him.

Joseph eats everything. He once ate one of the little blocks of blue disinfectant which hang inside the toilets. And he once ate a £50 note from his mother's wallet. And he eats string and rubber bands and tissues and writing paper and paints and plastic forks. Also he bangs his chin and screams a lot.

Tyrone said that there was a horse and a pig in the poo, so I said he was being stupid, but Siobhan said he wasn't. They were small plastic animals from the library that the staff use to make people tell stories. And Joseph had eaten them.

So I said I wasn't going to go into the toilets because there was poo on the floor and it made me feel uncomfortable to think about it, even though Mr. Ennison had come in and cleaned it up. And I wet my trousers and I had to put on some spare ones from the spare clothes locker in Mrs. Gascoyne's room. So Siobhan said I could use the staff room toilets for two days, but only two days, and then I would have to use the children's toilets again. And we made this a deal.

On the second, third and fourth days, which were Thursday, Friday and Saturday, nothing interesting happened.

On the fifth day, which was a Sunday, it rained very hard. I like it when it rains hard. It sounds like white noise everywhere, which is like silence but not empty.

I went upstairs and sat in my room and watched the water falling in the street. It was falling so hard that it looked like white sparks (and this is a simile, too, not a metaphor). And there was no one around because everyone was staying indoors. And it made me think how all the water in the world was connected, and this water had evaporated from the oceans somewhere in the middle of the Gulf of Mexico or Baffin Bay, and now it was falling in front of the house and it would drain away into the gutters and flow to a sewage station where it would be cleaned and then it would go into a river and go back into the ocean again.

And in the evening on Monday Father got a phone call from a lady whose cellar had flooded and he had to go out and fix it in an emergency.

If there is only one emergency Rhodri goes and fixes it because his wife and his children went to live in Somerset, which means he doesn't have anything to do in the evenings apart from playing snooker and drinking and watching the television, and he needs to do overtime to earn money to send to his wife to help her look after the children. And Father has me to look after. But this evening there were two emergencies, so Father told me to behave and to ring him on his mobile phone if there was a problem, and then he went out in the van.

So I went into his bedroom and opened up the cupboard and lifted the toolbox off the top of the shirt box and opened the shirt box.

I counted the letters. There were 43 of them. They were all addressed to me in the same handwriting.

I took one out and opened it.

Inside was this letter

3rd May   *451c Chapter Road*
                                                    London NW2 5NG
                                                    0208 887 8907

Dear Christopher,

We have a new fridge and cooker at last! Roger and I drove to the tip at the weekend to throw the old ones away. It's where people throw everything away. There are huge bins for three differant colours of bottles and cardboard and engine oil and garden waste and household waist and larger items (that's where we put the old fridge and cooker).

Then we went to a secondhand shop and bought a new cooker and a new fridge. Now the house feels a little bit more like home.

I was looking through some old photos last night, which made me sad. Then I found a photo of you playing with the train set we bought for you a couple of Christmas's ago. And that made me happy because it was one of the really good times we had together.

Do you remember how you played with it all day and you refused to go to bed at night because you were still playing with it. And do you remember how we told you about train timetabels and you made a train timetabel and you had a clock and you made the trains run on time. And there was a little woodden station, too, and we showed you how people who wanted to go on the train went to the station and bought a ticket and then got on the train? And then we got out a map and we showed you the little lines which were the trains lines connecting all the stations. And you played with it for weeks and weeks and weeks and we bought you more trains and you knew where they were all going.

I liked remembering that a lot.

I have to go now. It's half past three in the afternoon. I know you always like to know exactly what time it is. And I have to go to the Co-op and buy some ham to make Roger's tea with. I'll put this letter in the post box on the way to the shop.

Love,
Your Mum
x x x x x x

Then I opened another envelope. This was the letter that was inside

Flat 1, 312 Lausanne Rd
London N8 5BV
0208 756 4321

Dear Christopher,

I said that I wanted to explain to you why I went away when I had the time to do it properly. Now I have lots of time. So I'm sitting on the sofa here with this letter and the radio on and I'm going to try and explain.

I was not a very good mother, Christopher. Maybe if things had been different, maybe if you'd been differant, I might have been better at it. But that's just the way things turned out.

I'm not like your father. Your father is a much more pacient person. He just gets on with things and if things upset him he doesn't let it show. But that's not the way I am and there's nothing I can do to change that.

Do you remember once when we were shopping in town together? And we went into Bentalls and it was really crowded and we had to get a Christmas present for Grandma? And you were frightened because of all the people in the shop. It was the middle of Christmas shopping when everyone was in town. And I was talking to Mr. Land who works on the kichen floor and went to school with me. And you crouched down on the floor and put your hands over your ears and you were in the way of everyone. So I got cross, because I don't like shopping at Christmas, either, and I told you to behave and I tried to pick you up and move you. But you shouted and you knocked those mixers off the shelf and there was a big crash. And everyone turned round to see what was going on. And Mr. Land was realy nice about it but there were boxes and bits of broken bowl on the floor and everyone was staring and I saw that you had wet yourself and I was so cross and I wanted to take you out of the shop but you wouldn't let me touch you and you just lay on the floor and screamed and banged your hands and feet on the floor and the maniger came and asked what the problem was and I was at the end of my tether and I had to pay for two broken mixers and we just had to wait until you stoped screaming. And then I had to walk you all the way home which took hours because I knew you wouldn't go on the bus again.

And I remember that night I just cried and cried and cried and your father was really nice about it at first and he made you supper and he put you to bed and he said these things happen and it would be OK. But I said I couldn't take it anymore and eventually he got really cross and he told me I was being stupid and said I should pull myself together and I hit him, which was wrong, but I was so upset.

We had a lot of argumants like that. Because I often thought I couldn't take any more. And your father is really pacient but I'm not, I get cross, even though I don't mean too. And by the end we stopped talking to each other very much because we knew it would always end up in an argumant and it would go nowere. And I felt realy lonley.

And that was when I started spending lots of time with Roger. I mean obviously we had always spent lots of time with Roger and Eileen. But I started seeing Roger on his own because I could talk to him. He was the only person I could really talk to. And when I was with him I didn't feel lonley anymore.

And I know you might not understand any of this, but I

wanted to try to explain, so that you knew. And even if you don't understand now, you can keep this letter and read it later and maybe you might understand then.

And Roger told me that he and Eileen weren't in love with one another anymore, and that they hadn't been in love with one another for a long time. Which meant that he was feeling lonely too. So we had a lot in common. And then we realized that we were in love with one another. And he suggested that I should leave your father and that we should move into a house together. But I said that I couldn't leave you, and he was sad about that but he understood that you were realy important to me.

And then you and me had that argumant. Do you remember? It was about your supper one evening. I'd cooked you something and you wouldn't eat it. And you hadn't eaten for days and days and you were looking so thin. And you started to shout and I got cross and I threw the food across the room. Which I know I shouldn't have done. And you grabbed the chopping board and you threw that and it hit my foot and broke my toes. Then, of course, we had to go to the hospital and I had that plaster put on my foot. And afterward, at home, your father and I had a huge argumant. He blamed me for getting cross with you. And he said I should just give you what you wanted, even if it was just a plate of lettuce or a strawberry milk shake. And I said I was just trying to get you to eat something healthy. And he said you couldn't help it. And I said well I couldn't help it either and I just lost my rag. And he said that if he could keep his temper then I should bloody well keep my temper. And it went on and on like this.

And I couldn't walk properly for a month, do you remember, and your father had to look after you. And I remember looking at the two of you and seeing you together and thinking how you were *really differant with him. Much calmer. And you didn't shout at one another. And it made me so sad because it was like you didn't really need me at all. And somehow that was even worse than you and me arguing all the time because it was like I was invisible.*

And I think that was when I realized you and your father were probably better off if I wasn't living in the house. Then he would only have one person to look after instead of two.

Then Roger said that he had asked the bank for a transfer. That means he asked them if he could have a job in London, and he was leaving. He asked me if I wanted to come with him. I thought about it for a long time, Christopher. Honestly, I did. And it broke my heart, but eventualy I decided it would be better for all of us if I went. So I said yes.

I meant to say goodbye. I was going to come back and pick up some clothes when you were back from school. And that was when I was going to explain what I was doing and say that I would come back and see you as often as I could and you could come down to London sometimes to stay with us. But when I rang your father he said I couldn't come back. He was really angry. He said I couldn't talk to you. I didn't know what to do. He said that I was being self-ish and that I was never to set foot inside the house again. So I haven't. But I have written you these letters instead.

I wonder if you can understand any of this. I know it will be very difficult for you. But I hope you can understand a little.

Christopher, I never meant to hurt you. I thought that what I was doing was the best for all of us. I hope it is. And I want you to know that this is not your fault.

I used to have dreams that everything would get better. Do you remember, you used to say that you wanted to be an astranaut? Well, I used to have dreams where you were an astranaut and you were on the television and I thought that's my son. I wonder what it is that you want to be now. Has it changed? Are you still doing maths? I hope you are.

Please, Christopher, write to me sometime, or ring me on the telephone. The numbers at the top of the letter.

> *Love and kisses,*
> *Your Mother*
> *x x x x x x*

Then I opened a third envelope. This was the letter that was inside

18th September

Flat 1
312 Lausanne Road
London N8
0208 756 4321

Dear Christopher,

Well, I said I'd write to you every week, and I have. In fact, this is the second letter this week, so I'm doing even better than I said.

I have got a job! I'm working in Camden, at Perkin and Rashid, which is a Chartered Survayors. That means they go around looking at houses and work out how much they should cost and what work needs to be done on them and how much that work will cost. And also they work out how much new houses and offices and factories will cost to build.

It's a nice office. The other secretary is Angie. Her desk is covered in little teddy bears and furry toys and pictures of her children (so I've put a picture of you in a frame on my desk). She's really nice and we always go out for lunch together.

I don't know how long I'll stay here, though. I have to do a lot of adding up of numbers for when we send bills out to clients and I'm not very good at doing this (you'd be better at it than I am!).

The company is run by two men called Mr. Perkin and Mr. Rashid. Mr. Rashid is from Pakistan and very stern and always wants us to work faster. And Mr. Perkin is weird (Angie calls him Pervy Perkin). When he comes and stands next to me to ask a question he always puts his hand on my sholder and squots down so his face is really near mine and I can smell his toothpaste which gives me the creeps. And the pay is not very good, either. So I shall be looking for something better as soon as I get the chance.

I went up to Alexandra Palace the other day. It's a big park just round the corner from our flat, and the park is a huge hill with a big conference center on the top and it made me think of you because if you came here we could go there and fly kites or watch the planes coming into Heathrow airport and I know you'd like that.

I have to go now, Christopher. I'm writing this in my lunch hour (Angie is off sick with the flu, so we can't have lunch together). Please write to me sometime and tell me about how you are and what your doing at school.

I hope you got the present I sent you. Have you solved it yet. Roger and I saw it in a shop in Camden market and I know you've always liked puzles. Roger tried to get the two pieces apart before we wrapped it up and he couldn't do it. He said that if you managed to do it you were a genius.

Loads and loads of love,
Your Mother

x x x x

And this was the fourth letter

23rd August   *Flat 1*
                                                        312 Lausanne Road
                                                             London N8

Dear Christopher,

I'm sorry I didn't write last week. I had to go to the dentist and have two of my molars out. You might not remember when we had to take you to the dentist. You wouldn't let anyone put their hand inside your mouth so we had to put you to sleep so that the dentist could take one of your teeth out. Well, they didn't put me to sleep, they just gave me what is called a local anathsetic which means that you can't feel anything in your mouth, which is just as well because they had to saw through the bone to get the tooth out. And it didn't hurt at all. In fact I was laughing because the dentist had to tug and pull and strain so much and it seemed really funny to me. But when I got home the pain started to come back and I had to lie on the sofa for two days and take lots of painkillers…

Then I stopped reading the letter because I felt sick.

Mother had not had a heart attack. Mother had not died. Mother had been alive all the time. And Father had lied about this.

I tried really hard to think if there was any other explanation but I couldn't think of one. And then I couldn't think of anything at all because my brain wasn't working properly.

I felt giddy. It was like the room was swinging from side to side, as if it was at the top of a really tall building and the building was swinging backward and forward in a strong wind (this is a simile, too). But I knew that the room couldn't be swinging backward and forward, so it must have been something which was happening inside my head.

I rolled onto the bed and curled up in a ball.

My stomach hurt.

I don't know what happened then because there is a gap in my memory, like a bit of the tape had been erased. But I know that a lot of time must have passed because later on, when I opened my eyes again, I could see that it was dark outside the window. And I had been sick because there was sick all over the bed and on my hands and arms and face.

But before this I heard Father coming into the house and calling out my name, which is another reason why I know a lot of time had passed.

And it was strange because he was calling, "Christopher . . . ? Christopher . . . ?" and I could see my name written out as he was saying it. Often I can see what someone is saying written out like it is being printed on a computer screen, especially if they are in another room. But this was not on a computer screen. I could see it written really large, like it was on a big advert on the side of a bus. And it was in my mother's handwriting, like this

Christopher Christopher

And then I heard Father come up the stairs and walk into the room.

He said, "Christopher, what the hell are you doing?"

And I could tell that he was in the room, but his voice sounded tiny and far away, like people's voices sometimes do when I am groaning and I don't want them to be near me.

And he said, "What the fuck are you . . . ? That's my cupboard, Christopher. Those are . . . Oh shit . . . Shit, shit, shit, shit, shit."

Then he said nothing for a while.

Then he put his hand on my shoulder and moved me onto my side and he said, "Oh Christ." But it didn't hurt when he touched me, like it normally does. I could see him touching me, like I was watching a film of what was happening in the room, but I could hardly feel his hand at all. It was just like the wind blowing against me.

And then he was silent again for a while.

Then he said, "I'm sorry, Christopher. I'm so, so sorry."

Then he said, "You read the letters."

Then I could hear that he was crying because his breath sounded all bubbly and wet, like it does when someone has a cold and they have lots of snot in their nose.

Then he said, "I did it for your good, Christopher. Honestly I did. I never meant to lie. I just thought . . . I just thought it was better if you didn't know . . . that . . . that . . . I didn't mean to . . . I was going to show them to you when you were older."

Then he was silent again.

Then he said, "It was an accident."

Then he was silent again.

Then he said, "I didn't know what to say . . . I was in such a mess . . . She left a note and . . . Then she rang and . . . I said she was in hospital because . . . because I didn't know how to explain. It was so complicated. So difficult. And I . . . I said she was in hospital. And I know it wasn't true. But once I'd said that . . . I couldn't . . . I couldn't change it. Do you understand . . . Christopher . . . ? Christopher . . . ? It just . . . It got out of control and I wish . . ."

Then he was silent for a really long time.

Then he touched me on the shoulder again and said, "Christopher, we have to get you cleaned up, OK?"

He shook my shoulder a little bit but I didn't move.

And he said, "Christopher, I'm going to go to the bathroom and I'm going to run you a hot bath. Then I'm going to come back and take you to the bathroom, OK? Then I can put the sheets into the washing machine."

Then I heard him get up and go to the bathroom and turn the taps on. I listened to the water running into the bath. He didn't come back for a while. Then he came back and touched my shoulder again and said, "Let's do this really gently, Christopher. Let's sit you up and get your clothes off and get you into the bath, OK? I'm going to have to touch you, but it's going to be all right."

Then he lifted me up and made me sit on the side of the bed. He took my jumper and my shirt off and put them on the bed. Then he made me stand up and walk through to the bathroom. And I didn't scream. And I didn't fight. And I didn't hit him.

163.   When I was little and I first went to school, my main teacher was called Julie, because Siobhan hadn't started working at the school then. She only started working at the school when I was twelve.

And one day Julie sat down at a desk next to me and put a tube of Smarties on the desk, and she said, "Christopher, what do you think is in here?"

And I said, "Smarties."

Then she took the top off the Smarties tube and turned it

upside down and a little red pencil came out and she laughed and I said, "It's not Smarties, it's a pencil."

Then she put the little red pencil back inside the Smarties tube and put the top back on.

Then she said, "If your mummy came in now and we asked her what was inside the Smarties tube, what do you think she would say?" because I used to call Mother *Mummy* then, not *Mother*.

And I said, "A pencil."

That was because when I was little I didn't understand about other people having minds. And Julie said to Mother and Father that I would always find this very difficult. But I don't find this difficult now. Because I decided that it was a kind of puzzle, and if something is a puzzle there is always a way of solving it.

It's like computers. People think computers are different from people because they don't have minds, even though, in the Turing test, computers can have conversations with people about the weather and wine and what Italy is like, and they can even tell jokes.

But the mind is just a complicated machine.

And when we look at things we think we're just looking out of our eyes like we're looking out of little windows and there's a person inside our head, but we're not. We're looking at a screen inside our heads, like a computer screen.

And you can tell this because of an experiment which I saw on TV in a series called *How the Mind Works.* And in this experiment you put your head in a clamp and you look at a page of writing on a screen. And it looks like a normal page of writing and nothing is changing. But after a while, as your eye moves round the page, you realize that something is very strange because when you try to read a bit of the page you've read before it's different.

And this is because when your eye flicks from one point to another you don't see anything at all and you're blind. And the flicks are called *saccades*. Because if you saw everything when your eye flicked from one point to another you'd feel giddy. And in the experiment there is a sensor which tells when your eye is flicking from one place to another, and when it's doing this it changes some of the words on the page in a place where you're not looking.

But you don't notice that you're blind during saccades because your brain fills in the screen in your head to make it seem like you're looking out of two little windows in your head. And you don't notice that words have changed on another part of the page because your mind fills in a picture of things you're not looking at at that moment.

And people are different from animals because they can have pictures on the screens in their heads of things which they are not looking at. They can have pictures of someone in another room. Or they can have a picture of what is going to happen tomorrow. Or they can have pictures of themselves as an astronaut. Or they can have pictures of really big numbers. Or they can have pictures of Chains of Reasoning when they're trying to work something out.

And that is why a dog can go to the vet and have a really big operation and have metal pins sticking out of its leg but if it sees a cat it forgets that it has pins sticking out of its leg and chases after the cat. But when a person has an operation it has a picture in its head of the hurt carrying on for months and months. And it has a picture of all the stitches in its leg and the broken bone and the pins and even if it sees a bus it has to catch it doesn't run because it has a picture in its head of the bones crunching together and the stitches breaking and even more pain.

And that is why people think that computers don't have minds, and why people think that their brains are special, and different from computers. Because people can see the screen inside their head and they think there is someone in their head sitting there looking at the screen, like Captain Jean-Luc Picard in *Star Trek: The Next Generation* sitting in his captain's seat looking at a big screen. And they think that this person is their special human mind, which is called a *homunculus*, which means *a little man*. And they think that computers don't have this homunculus.

But this homunculus is just another picture on the screen in their heads. And when the homunculus is on the screen in their heads (because the person is thinking about the homunculus) there is another bit of the brain watching the screen. And when the person thinks about this part of the brain (the bit that is watching the homunculus on the screen) they put this bit of the brain on the screen and there is another bit of the brain watching the screen. But the brain doesn't see this happen because it is like the eye flicking from one place to another and people are blind inside their heads when they do the changing from thinking about one thing to thinking about another.

And this is why people's brains are like computers. And it's not because they are special but because they have to keep turning off for fractions of a second while the screen changes. And because there is something they can't see people think it has to be special, because people always think there is something special about what they can't see, like the dark side of the moon, or the other side of a black hole, or in the dark when they wake up at night and they're scared.

Also people think they're not computers because they have feelings and computers don't have feelings. But feelings are just having a picture on the screen in your head of what is going to happen tomorrow or next year, or what might have happened instead of what did happen, and if it is a happy picture they smile and if it is a sad picture they cry.

167.   After Father had given me a bath and cleaned the sick off me and dried me off with a towel, he took me to my bedroom and put some clean clothes on.

Then he said, "Have you had anything to eat yet this evening?"

But I didn't say anything.

Then he said, "Can I get you anything to eat, Christopher?"

But I still didn't say anything.

So he said, "OK. Look. I'm going to go and put your clothes and the bedsheets into the washing machine and then I'll come back, OK?"

I sat on the bed and looked at my knees.

So Father went out of the room and picked up my clothes from the bathroom floor and put them on the landing. Then he went and got the sheets from his bed and brought them out onto the landing together with my shirt and my jumper. Then he picked them all up and took them downstairs. Then I heard him start the washing machine and I heard the boiler starting up and the water in the water pipes going into the washing machine.

That was all I could hear for a long time.

I doubled 2's in my head because it made me feel calmer. I got to 33554432, which is 2^{25}, which was not very much because I've got to 2^{45} before, but my brain wasn't working very well.

Then Father came back into the room again and said, "How are you feeling? Can I get you anything?"

I didn't say anything. I carried on looking at my knees.

And Father didn't say anything either. He just sat down on the bed next to me and put his elbows on his knees and looked down at the carpet between his legs where there was a little red piece of Lego with eight nobbles on.

Then I heard Toby waking up, because he is nocturnal, and I heard him rustling in his cage.

And Father was silent for a really long time.

Then he said, "Look, maybe I shouldn't say this, but . . . I want you to know that you can trust me. And . . . OK, maybe I don't tell the truth all the time. God knows, I try, Christopher, God knows I do, but . . . Life is difficult, you know. It's bloody hard telling the truth all the time. Sometimes it's impossible. And I want you to know that I'm trying, I really am. And perhaps this is not a very good time to say this, and I know you're not going to like it, but . . . You have to know that I am going to tell you the truth from now on. About everything. Because . . . if you don't tell the truth now, then later on . . . later on it hurts even more. So . . ."

Father rubbed his face with his hands and pulled his chin down with his fingers and stared at the wall. I could see him out of the corner of my eye.

And he said, "I killed Wellington, Christopher."

I wondered if this was a joke, because I don't understand jokes, and when people tell jokes they don't mean what they say.

But then Father said, "Please. Christopher. Just . . . let me explain." Then he sucked in some air and he said, "When your mum left . . . Eileen . . . Mrs. Shears . . . she was very good to us. Very good to me. She helped me through a very difficult time. And I'm not sure I would have made it without her. Well, you know how she was round here most days. Helping out with the cooking and the cleaning. Popping over to see if we were OK, if we needed anything . . . I thought . . . Well . . . Shit, Christopher, I'm trying to keep this simple . . . I thought she might carry on coming over. I thought . . . and maybe I was being stupid . . . I thought she might . . . eventually . . . want to move in here. Or that we might move into her house. We . . . we got on really, really well. I thought we were friends. And I guess I thought wrong. I guess . . . in the end . . . it comes down to . . . Shit . . . We argued, Christopher, and . . . She said some things I'm not going to say to you because they're not nice, but they hurt, but . . . I think she cared more for that bloody dog than for me, for us. And maybe that's not so stupid, looking back. Maybe we are a bloody handful. And maybe it is easier living on your own looking after some stupid mutt than sharing your life with other actual human beings. I mean, shit, buddy, we're not exactly low-maintenance, are we . . . ? Anyway, we had this row. Well, quite a few rows to be honest. But after this particularly nasty little blowout, she chucked me out of the house. And you know what that bloody dog was like after the operation. Bloody schizophrenic. Nice as pie one moment, roll over, tickle its stomach. Sink its teeth into your leg the next. Anyway, we're yelling at each other and it's in the garden relieving itself. So when she slams the door behind me the bugger's waiting for me. And . . . I know, I know. Maybe if I'd just given it a kick it would probably have backed off. But, shit, Christopher, when that red mist comes down . . .

Christ, you know how it is. I mean, we're not that different, me and you. And all I could think was that she cared more about this bloody dog than she did about you or me. And it was like everything I'd been bottling up for two years just . . ."

Then Father was silent for a bit.

Then he said, "I'm sorry, Christopher. I promise you, I never meant for it to turn out like this."

And then I knew that it wasn't a joke and I was really frightened.

Father said, "We all make mistakes, Christopher. You, me, your mum, everyone. And sometimes they're really big mistakes. We're only human."

Then he held up his right hand and spread his fingers out in a fan.

But I screamed and pushed him backward so that he fell off the bed and onto the floor.

He sat up and said, "OK. Look. Christopher. I'm sorry. Let's leave it for tonight, OK? I'm going to go downstairs and you get some sleep and we'll talk in the morning." Then he said, "It's going to be all right. Honestly. Trust me."

Then he stood up and took a deep breath and went out of the room.

I sat on the bed for a long time looking at the floor. Then I heard Toby scratching in his cage. I looked up and saw him staring through the bars at me.

I had to get out of the house. Father had murdered Wellington. That meant he could murder me, because I couldn't trust him, even though he had said "Trust me," because he had told a lie about a big thing.

But I couldn't get out of the house straightaway because he would see me, so I would have to wait until he was asleep.

The time was 11:16 p.m.

I tried doubling 2's again, but I couldn't get past 2^{15}, which was **32768.** So I groaned to make the time pass quicker and not think.

Then it was 1:20 a.m. but I hadn't heard Father come upstairs to bed. I wondered if he was asleep downstairs or whether he was waiting to come in and kill me. So I got out my Swiss Army knife and opened the saw blade so that I could defend myself. Then I went out of my bedroom really quietly and listened. I couldn't hear anything, so I started going downstairs really quietly and really slowly. And when I got downstairs I could see Father's foot through the door of the living room. I waited for 4 minutes to see if it moved, but it didn't move. So I carried on walking till I got to the hallway. Then I looked round the door of the living room.

Father was lying on the sofa with his eyes closed.

I looked at him for a long time.

Then he snored and I jumped and I could hear the blood in my ears and my heart going really fast and a pain like someone had blown up a really big balloon inside my chest.

I wondered if I was going to have a heart attack.

Father's eyes were still closed. I wondered if he was pretending to be asleep. So I gripped the penknife really hard and I knocked on the doorframe.

Father moved his head from one side to the other and his foot twitched and he said "Gnnnn," but his eyes stayed closed. And then he snored again.

He was asleep.

That meant I could get out of the house if I was really quiet so I didn't wake him up.

I took both my coats and my scarf from the hooks next to

the front door and I put them all on because it would be cold outside at night. Then I went upstairs again really quietly, but it was difficult because my legs were shaking. I went into my room and I picked up Toby's cage. He was making scratching noises, so I took off one of the coats and put it over the cage to make the noise quieter. Then I carried him downstairs again.

Father was still asleep.

I went into the kitchen and I picked up my special food box. I unlocked the back door and stepped outside. Then I held the handle of the door down as I shut it again so that the click wasn't too loud. Then I walked down the bottom of the garden.

At the bottom of the garden is a shed. It has the lawn mower and the hedge cutter in it, and lots of gardening equipment that Mother used to use, like pots and bags of compost and bamboo canes and string and spades. It would be a bit warmer in the shed but I knew that Father might look for me in the shed, so I went round the back of the shed and I squeezed into the gap between the wall of the shed and the fence, behind the big black plastic tub for collecting rainwater. Then I sat down and I felt a bit safer.

I decided to leave my other coat over Toby's cage because I didn't want him to get cold and die.

I opened up my special food box. Inside was the Milkybar and two licorice laces and three clementines and a pink wafer biscuit and my red food coloring. I didn't feel hungry but I knew that I should eat something because if you don't eat something you can get cold, so I ate two clementines and the Milkybar.

Then I wondered what I would do next.

173. Between the roof of the shed and the big plant that hangs over the fence from the house next door I could see the constellation **Orion.**

People say that **Orion** is called Orion because Orion was a hunter and the constellation looks like a hunter with a club and a bow and arrow, like this

But this is really silly because it is just stars, and you could join up the dots in any way you wanted, and you could make it look like a lady with an umbrella who is waving, or the coffeemaker which Mrs. Shears has, which is from Italy, with a handle and steam coming out, or like a dinosaur

And there aren't any lines in space, so you could join bits of **Orion** to bits of **Lepus** or **Taurus** or **Gemini** and say that they were a constellation called **the Bunch of Grapes** or **Jesus** or **the**

Bicycle (except that they didn't have bicycles in Roman and Greek times, which was when they called **Orion** Orion).

And anyway, **Orion** is not a hunter or a coffeemaker or a dinosaur. It is just Betelgeuse and Bellatrix and Alnilam and Rigel and 17 other stars I don't know the names of. And they are nuclear explosions billions of miles away.

And that is the truth.

179. I stayed awake until 3:47. That was the last time I looked at my watch before I fell asleep. It has a luminous face and lights up if you press a button, so I could read it in the dark. I was cold and I was frightened Father might come out and find me. But I felt safer in the garden because I was hidden.

I looked at the sky a lot. I like looking up at the sky in the garden at night. In summer I sometimes come outside at night with my torch and my planisphere, which is two circles of plastic with a pin through the middle. And on the bottom is a map of the sky and on top is an aperture which is an opening shaped in a parabola and you turn it round to see a map of the sky that you can see on that day of the year from the latitude 51.5° north, which is the latitude that Swindon is on, because the largest bit of the sky is always on the other side of the earth.

And when you look at the sky you know you are looking at stars which are hundreds and thousands of light-years away from you. And some of the stars don't even exist anymore because their light has taken so long to get to us that they are already dead, or they have exploded and collapsed into red dwarfs. And that makes you seem very small, and if you have difficult things in your life it is nice to think that they are what is called *negligible*, which means that they are so small you don't have to take them into account when you are calculating something.

I didn't sleep very well because of the cold and because the ground was very bumpy and pointy underneath me and because Toby was scratching in his cage a lot. But when I woke up properly it was dawn and the sky was all orange and blue and purple and I could hear birds singing, which is called *the Dawn Chorus*. And I stayed where I was for another 2 hours and 32 minutes, and then I heard Father come into the garden and call out, "Christopher . . . ? Christopher . . . ?"

So I turned round and I found an old plastic sack covered in mud that used to have fertilizer in it and I squeezed myself and Toby's cage and my special food box into the corner between the wall of the shed and the fence and the rainwater tub and I covered myself with the fertilizer sack. And then I heard Father coming down the garden and I took my Swiss Army knife out of my pocket and got out the saw blade and held it in case he found us. And I heard him open the door of the shed and look inside. And then I heard him say "Shit." And then I heard his footsteps in the bushes round the side of the shed and my heart was beating really fast and I could feel the feeling like a balloon inside my chest again and I think he might have looked round the back of the shed, but I couldn't see because I was hiding, but he didn't see me because I heard him walking back up the garden again.

Then I stayed still and I looked at my watch and I stayed still for 27 minutes. And then I heard Father start the engine of his van. I knew it was his van because I heard it very often and it was nearby and I knew it wasn't any of the neighbors' cars because the people who take drugs have a Volkswagen camper van and Mr. Thompson, who lives at number 40, has a Vauxhall Cavalier and the people who live at number 34 have a Peugeot and they all sound different.

And when I heard him drive away from the house I knew it would be safe to come out.

And then I had to decide what to do because I couldn't live in the house with Father anymore because it was dangerous.

So I made a decision.

I decided that I would go and knock on Mrs. Shears's door and I would go and live with her, because I knew her and she wasn't a stranger and I had stayed in her house before, when there was a power cut on our side of the street. And this time she wouldn't tell me to go away because I would be able to tell her who had killed Wellington and that way she would know that I was a friend. And also she would understand why I couldn't live with Father anymore.

I took the licorice laces and the pink wafer biscuit and the last clementine out of my special food box and put them in my pocket and hid the special food box under the fertilizer bag. Then I picked up Toby's cage and my extra coat and I climbed out from behind the shed. I walked up the garden and down the side of the house. I undid the bolt in the garden door and walked out in front of the house.

There was no one in the street so I crossed and walked up the drive to Mrs. Shears's house and knocked on the door and waited and worked out what I was going to say when she opened the door.

But she didn't come to the door. So I knocked again.

Then I turned round and saw some people walking down the street and I was frightened again because it was two of the people who take drugs in the house next door. So I grabbed Toby's cage and went round the side of Mrs. Shears's house and sat down behind the dustbin so they couldn't see me.

And then I had to work out what to do.

And I did this by thinking of all the things I could do and deciding whether they were the right decision or not.

I decided that I couldn't go home again.

And I decided that I couldn't go and live with Siobhan because she couldn't look after me when school was closed because she was a teacher and not a friend or a member of my family.

And I decided that I couldn't go and live with Uncle Terry because he lived in Sunderland and I didn't know how to get to Sunderland and I didn't like Uncle Terry because he smoked cigarettes and stroked my hair.

And I decided I couldn't go and live with Mrs. Alexander because she wasn't a friend or a member of my family even if she had a dog, because I couldn't stay overnight in her house or use her toilet because she had used it and she was a stranger.

And then I thought that I could go and live with Mother because she was my family and I knew where she lived because I could remember the address from the letters, which was 451c Chapter Road, London NW2 5NG. Except that she lived in London and I'd never been to London before. I'd only been to Dover to go to France, and to Sunderland to visit Uncle Terry and to Manchester to visit Aunt Ruth, who had cancer, except she didn't have cancer when I was there. And I had never been anywhere apart from the shop at the end of the road on my own. And the thought of going somewhere on my own was frightening.

But then I thought about going home again, or staying

where I was, or hiding in the garden every night and Father finding me, and that made me feel even more frightened. And when I thought about that I felt like I was going to be sick again like I did the night before.

And then I realized that there was nothing I could do which felt safe. And I made a picture of it in my head like this

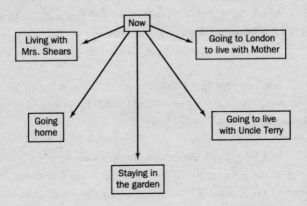

And then I imagined crossing out all the possibilities which were impossible, which is like in a maths exam when you look at all the questions and you decide which ones you are going to do and which ones you are not going to do and you cross out all the ones which you are not going to do because then your decision is final and you can't change your mind. And it was like this

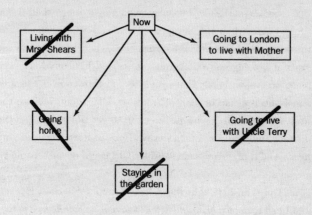

Which meant that I had to go to London to live with Mother. And I could do it by going on a train because I knew all about trains from the train set, how you looked at the timetable and went to the station and bought a ticket and looked at the departure board to see if your train was on time and then you went to the right platform and got on board. And I would go from Swindon station, where Sherlock Holmes and Doctor Watson stop for lunch when they are on their way to Ross from Paddington in *The Boscombe Valley Mystery.*

And then I looked at the wall on the opposite side of the little passage down the side of Mrs. Shears's house where I was sitting and there was the circular lid of a very old metal pan leaning against the wall. And it was covered in rust. And it looked like the surface of a planet because the rust was shaped like countries and continents and islands.

And then I thought how I could never be an astronaut because being an astronaut meant being hundreds of thousands of miles away from home, and my home was in London now and that was about 100 miles away, which was more than 1,000 times nearer than my home would be if I was in space, and thinking about this made me hurt. Like when I fell over in the grass at the edge of a playground once and I cut my knee on a piece of broken bottle that someone had thrown over the wall and I sliced a flap of skin off and Mr. Davis had to clean the flesh under the flap with disinfectant to get the germs and the dirt out and it hurt so much I cried. But this hurt was inside my head. And it made me sad to think that I could never become an astronaut.

And then I thought that I had to be like Sherlock Holmes and I had to *detach my mind at will to a remarkable degree* so that I did not notice how much it was hurting inside my head.

And then I thought I would need money if I was going to go to London. And I would need food to eat because it was a long journey and I wouldn't know where to get food from. And then I thought I would need someone to look after Toby when I went to London because I couldn't take him with me.

And then I *Formulated a Plan*. And that made me feel better because there was something in my head that had an order and a pattern and I just had to follow the instructions one after the other.

I stood up and I made sure there was no one in the street. Then I went to Mrs. Alexander's house, which is next door to Mrs. Shears's house, and I knocked on the door.

Then Mrs. Alexander opened the door, and she said, "Christopher, what on earth has happened to you?"

And I said, "Can you look after Toby for me?"

And she said, "Who's Toby?"

And I said, "Toby's my pet rat."

Then Mrs. Alexander said, "Oh . . . Oh yes. I remember now. You told me."

Then I held Toby's cage up and said, "This is him."

Mrs. Alexander took a step backward into her hallway.

And I said, "He eats special pellets and you can buy them from a pet shop. But he can also eat biscuits and carrots and bread and chicken bones. But you mustn't give him chocolate because it's got caffeine and theobromine in it, which are methylxanthines, and it's poisonous for rats in large quantities. And he needs new water in his bottle every day, too. And he won't mind being in someone else's house because he's an animal. And he likes to come out of his cage, but it doesn't matter if you don't take him out."

Then Mrs. Alexander said, "Why do you need someone to look after Toby, Christopher?"

And I said, "I'm going to London."

And she said, "How long are you going for?"

And I said, "Until I go to university."

And she said, "Can't you take Toby with you?"

And I said, "London's a long way away and I don't want to take him on the train because I might lose him."

And Mrs. Alexander said, "Right." And then she said, "Are you and your father moving house?"

And I said, "No."

And she said, "So, why are you going to London?"

And I said, "I'm going to live with Mother."

And she said, "I thought you told me your mother was dead."

And I said, "I thought she was dead, but she was still alive. And Father lied to me. And also he said he killed Wellington."

And Mrs. Alexander said, "Oh, my goodness."

And I said, "I'm going to live with my mother because Father killed Wellington and he lied and I'm frightened of being in the house with him."

And Mrs. Alexander said, "Is your mother here?"

And I said, "No. Mother is in London."

And she said, "So you're going to London on your own?"

And I said, "Yes."

And she said, "Look, Christopher, why don't you come inside and sit down and we can talk about this and work out what is the best thing to do."

And I said, "No. I can't come inside. Will you look after Toby for me?"

And she said, "I really don't think that would be a good idea, Christopher."

And I didn't say anything.

And she said, "Where's your father at the moment, Christopher?"

And I said, "I don't know."

And she said, "Well, perhaps we should try and give him a ring and see if we can get in touch with him. I'm sure he's worried about you. And I'm sure that there's been some dreadful misunderstanding."

So I turned round and I ran across the road back to our house. And I didn't look before I crossed the road and a yellow Mini had to stop and the tires squealed on the road. And I ran down the side of the house and back through the garden gate and I bolted it behind me.

I tried to open the kitchen door but it was locked. So I picked up a brick that was lying on the ground and I smashed it through the window and the glass shattered everywhere. Then I put my arm through the broken glass and I opened the door from the inside.

I went into the house and I put Toby down on the kitchen table. Then I ran upstairs and I grabbed my schoolbag and I put some food for Toby in it and some of my maths books and some clean pants and a vest and a clean shirt. Then I came downstairs and I opened the fridge and I put a carton of orange juice into my bag, and a bottle of milk that hadn't been opened. And I took two more clementines and two tins of baked beans and a packet of custard creams from the cupboard and I put them in my bag as well, because I could open them with the can opener or my Swiss Army knife.

Then I looked on the surface next to the sink and I saw Father's mobile phone and his wallet and his address book and I felt *my skin...cold under my clothes* like Doctor Watson in *The Sign of Four* when he sees the tiny footsteps of Tonga, the Andaman Islander, on the roof of Bartholomew Sholto's house in Norwood, because I thought Father had come back and he was in the house, and the pain in my head got much worse. But then I rewound the pictures in my memory and I saw that his van wasn't parked outside the house, so he must have left his mobile phone and his wallet and his address book when he left the house. And I picked up his wallet and I took his bank card out because that was how I could get money because the card has a PIN which is the secret code which you put into the machine at the bank to get money out and Father hadn't written it down in a safe place, which is what you're meant to do, but he had told me because he said I'd never forget it. And it was 3558. And I put the card into my pocket.

Then I took Toby out of his cage and put him into the pocket of one of my coats because the cage was very heavy to carry all the way to London. And then I went out of the kitchen door into the garden again.

I went out through the garden gate and made sure there wasn't anyone watching, and then I started walking toward the school because that was a direction I knew, and when I got to school I could ask Siobhan where the train station was.

Normally I would have got more and more frightened if I was walking to school, because I had never done it before. But I was frightened in two different ways. And one way was being frightened of being far away from a place I was used to, and the other was being frightened of being near where Father lived, and they were *in inverse proportion to one another*, so that the total fear remained a constant as I got further away from home and further away from Father like this

$$\text{Fear}_\text{total} \approx \text{Fear}_\text{new place} \times \text{Fear}_\text{near Father} \approx \text{constant}$$

It takes 19 minutes for the bus to get to school from our house, but it took me 47 minutes to walk the same distance, so I was very tired when I got there and I hoped that I could stay at school for a little while and have some biscuits and some orange juice before I went to the train station. But I couldn't, because when I got to the school I saw that Father's van was parked outside in the car park. And I knew it was his van because it said **Ed Boone Heating Maintenance & Boiler Repair** on the side with a crossed spanners sign like this

And when I saw the van I was sick again. But I knew I was going to be sick this time so I didn't sick all over myself and I was just sick onto the wall and the pavement, and there wasn't very much sick because I hadn't eaten much. And when I had been sick I wanted to curl up on the ground and do groaning. But I knew that if I curled up on the ground and did groaning, then Father would come out of the school and he would see me and he would catch me and take me home. So I took lots of deep breaths like Siobhan says I have to do if someone hits me at school, and I counted 50 breaths and I concentrated very hard on the numbers and did their cubes as I said them. And that made the hurt less painful.

And then I cleaned the sick away from my mouth and I made a decision that I would have to find out how to get to the train station and I would do this by asking someone, and it would be a lady because when they talked to us about Stranger Danger at school they say that if a man comes up to you and talks to you and you feel frightened you should call out and find a lady to run to because ladies are safer.

So I got out my Swiss Army knife and I flicked out the saw blade and I held it tightly in the pocket that Toby wasn't in so that I could stab someone if they grabbed hold of me, and then I saw a lady on the other side of the street with a baby in a pushchair and a little boy with a toy elephant, so I decided to ask her. And this time I looked left and right and left again so that I wouldn't be run over by a car, and I crossed the road.

And I said to the lady, "Where can I buy a map?"

And she said, "Pardon?"

And I said, "Where can I buy a map?" And I could feel the hand that was holding the knife shaking even though I wasn't shaking it.

And she said, "Patrick, put that down, it's dirty. A map of where?"

And I said, "A map of here."

And she said, "I don't know." And then she said, "Where do you want to get to?"

And I said, "I'm going to the train station."

And she laughed and she said, "You don't need a map to get to the train station."

And I said, "I do, because I don't know where the train station is."

And she said, "You can see it from here."

And I said, "No I can't. And also I need to know where there is a cash machine."

And she pointed and said, "There. That building. Says *Signal Point* on the top. There's a British Rail sign on the other end. The station's at the bottom of that. Patrick, if I've told you once, I've told you a thousand times. Don't pick things off the pavement and stick them in your mouth."

And I looked and I could see a building with writing at the top, but it was a long way away so it was hard to read, and I said, "Do you mean the stripy building with the horizontal windows?"

And she said, "That's the one."

And I said, "How do I get to that building?"

And she said, "Gordon Bennett." And then she said, "Follow that bus," and she pointed to a bus that was going past.

So I started to run. But buses go really fast and I had to make sure that Toby didn't fall out of my pocket. But I managed to keep running after the bus for a long way and I crossed 6 side roads before it turned down another street and I couldn't see it anymore.

And then I stopped running because I was breathing really hard and my legs hurt. And I was in a street with lots of shops. And I remembered being in this street when I went shopping with Mother. And there were lots of people in the street doing their shopping, but I didn't want them to touch me, so I walked at the edge of the road. And I didn't like all the people being near me and all the noise because it was too much information in my head and it made it hard to think, like there was shouting in my head. So I put my hands over my ears and I groaned very quietly.

And then I noticed that I could still see the ⇌ sign that the lady had pointed at, so I kept on walking toward it.

And then I couldn't see the ⇌ sign anymore. And I had forgotten to remember where it was, and this was frightening because I was lost and because I do not forget things. And normally I would make a map in my head and I would follow the map and I would be a little cross on the map that showed where I was, but there was too much interference in my head and this had made me confused. So I stood under the green and white canvas roof outside a greengrocer's shop where there were carrots and onions and parsnips and broccoli in boxes that had a plastic furry green carpet in them, and I made a plan.

I knew that the train station was somewhere near. And if something is nearby you can find it by moving in a spiral, walking clockwise and taking every right turn until you come back to a road you've already walked on, then taking the next left, then taking every right turn and so on, like this (but this is a hypothetical diagram, too, and not a map of Swindon)

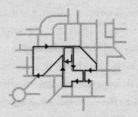

And that was how I found the train station, and I concentrated really hard on following the rules and making a map of the center of the town in my head as I walked, and that way it was easier to ignore all the people and all the noise around me.

And then I went into the train station.

181.   I see everything.

That is why I don't like new places. If I am in a place I know, like home, or school, or the bus, or the shop, or the street, I have seen almost everything in it beforehand and all I have to do is to look at the things that have changed or moved. For example, one week the **Shakespeare's Globe** poster had fallen down in the classroom at school and you could tell because it had been put back slightly to the right and there were three little circles of Blu-Tack stain on the wall down the left-hand side of the poster. And the next day someone had graffitied **CROW APTOK** to lamppost 437 in our street, which is the one outside number 35.

But most people are lazy. They never look at everything. They do what is called *glancing*, which is the same word for bumping off something and carrying on in almost the same direction, e.g., when a snooker ball glances off another snooker ball. And the information in their head is really simple. For example, if they are in the countryside, it might be

1. I am standing in a field that is full of grass.

2. There are some cows in the fields.

3. It is sunny with a few clouds.

4. There are some flowers in the grass.

5. There is a village in the distance.

6. There is a fence at the edge of the field and it has a gate in it.

And then they would stop noticing anything because they would be thinking something else like, "Oh, it is very beautiful here," or "I'm worried that I might have left the gas cooker on," or "I wonder if Julie has given birth yet."[12]

But if I am standing in a field in the countryside I notice everything. For example, I remember standing in a field on Wednesday, 15 June 1994, because Father and Mother and I were driving to Dover to get a ferry to France and we did what Father called *Taking the Scenic Route*, which means going by little roads and stopping for lunch in a pub garden, and I had to stop to go for a wee, and I went into a field with cows in it and after I'd had a wee I stopped and looked at the field and I noticed these things

1. There are 19 cows in the field, 15 of which are black and white and 4 of which are brown and white.

2. There is a village in the distance which has 31 visible houses and a church with a square tower and not a spire.

3. There are ridges in the field, which means that in medieval times it was what is called a *ridge and*

---

[12] This is really true because I asked Siobhan what people thought about when they looked at things, and this is what she said.

furrow field and people who lived in the village would have a ridge each to do farming on.

4. There is an old plastic bag from Asda in the hedge, and a squashed Coca-Cola can with a snail on it, and a long piece of orange string.

5. The northeast corner of the field is highest and the southwest corner is lowest (I had a compass because we were going on holiday and I wanted to know where Swindon was when we were in France) and the field is folded downward slightly along the line between these two corners so that the northwest and southeast corners are slightly lower than they would be if the field was an inclined plane.

6. I can see three different types of grass and two colors of flowers in the grass.

7. The cows are mostly facing uphill.

And there were 31 more things in this list of things I noticed but Siobhan said I didn't need to write them all down. And it means that it is very tiring if I am in a new place because I see all these things, and if someone asked me afterward what the cows looked like, I could ask which one, and I could do a drawing of them at home and say that a particular cow had patterns on it like this

And I realize that I told a lie in **Chapter 13** because I said "I cannot tell jokes," because I do know 3 jokes that I can tell and

I understand and one of them is about a cow, and Siobhan said I didn't have to go back and change what I wrote in **Chapter 13** because it doesn't matter because it is not a lie, just a *clarification*.

And this is the joke.

There are three men on a train. One of them is an economist and one of them is a logician and one of them is a mathematician. And they have just crossed the border into Scotland (I don't know why they are going to Scotland) and they see a brown cow standing in a field from the window of the train (and the cow is standing parallel to the train).

And the economist says, "Look, the cows in Scotland are brown."

And the logician says, "No. There are cows in Scotland of which one at least is brown."

And the mathematician says, "No. There is at least one cow in Scotland, of which one side appears to be brown."

And it is funny because economists are not real scientists, and because logicians think more clearly, but mathematicians are best.

And when I am in a new place, because I see everything, it is like when a computer is doing too many things at the same time and the central processor unit is blocked up and there isn't any space left to think about other things. And when I am in a new place and there are lots of people there it is even harder because people are not like cows and flowers and grass and they can talk to you and do things that you don't expect, so you have to notice everything that is in the place, and also you have to notice things that might happen as well. And sometimes when I am in a new place and there are lots of people there it is like a computer crashing and I have to close my eyes and put my hands over my ears and groan, which is like pressing CTRL + ALT +

DEL and shutting down programs and turning the computer off and rebooting so that I can remember what I am doing and where I am meant to be going.

And that is why I am good at chess and maths and logic, because most people are almost blind and they don't see most things and there is lots of spare capacity in their heads and it is filled with things which aren't connected and are silly, like, "I'm worried that I might have left the gas cooker on."

191. My train set had a little building that was two rooms with a corridor between them, and one was the ticket office where you bought the tickets, and one was a waiting room where you waited for the train. But the train station in Swindon wasn't like that. It was a tunnel and some stairs, and a shop and café and a waiting room like this

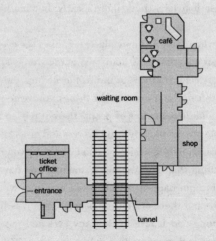

But this is not a very accurate map of the station because I was scared so I was not noticing things very well, and this is just what I remember so it is an *approximation*.

And it was like standing on a cliff in a really strong wind because it made me feel giddy and sick because there were lots of people walking into and out of the tunnel and it was really echoey and there was only one way to go and that was down the tunnel, and it smelled of toilets and cigarettes. So I stood against the wall and held on to the edge of a sign that said **Customers seeking access to car park please use assistance phone opposite, right of the ticket office** to make sure that I didn't fall over and go into a crouch on the ground. And I wanted to go home but I was frightened of going home and I tried to make a plan of what I should do in my head but there were too many things to look at and too many things to hear.

So I put my hands over my ears to block out the noise and think. And I thought that I had to stay in the station to get on a train and I had to sit down somewhere and there was nowhere to sit down near the door of the station so I had to walk down the tunnel. So I said to myself, in my head, not out loud, "I will walk down the tunnel and there might be somewhere I can sit down and then I can shut my eyes and I can think," and I walk down the tunnel trying to concentrate on the sign at the end of the tunnel that said **WARNING CCTV in operation.** And it was like stepping off the cliff on a tightrope.

And eventually I got to the end of the tunnel and there were some stairs and I went up the stairs and there were still lots of people and I groaned and there was a shop at the top of the stairs and a room with chairs in it but there were too many people in the room with chairs in it, so I walked past it. And there were signs saying **Great Western** and **cold beers and lagers** and CAUTION WET FLOOR and **Your 50p will keep a premature baby alive for 1.8 seconds** and **transforming travel** and **Refreshingly Different** and IT'S DELICIOUS IT'S CREAMY AND IT'S ONLY £1.30 HOT CHOC DELUXE and **0870 777 7676** and **The Lemon Tree** and **No Smoking** and FINE TEAS and there were some little tables with chairs next to them and no one was sitting at one of the tables and it was in a corner and I sat down on one of the chairs next to it and I closed my eyes. And I put my hands in my pockets and Toby climbed into my hand and I gave him two pellets of rat food from my bag and I gripped the Swiss Army knife in the other hand, and I groaned to cover up the noise because I had taken my hands off my ears, but not so loud that other people would hear me groaning and come and talk to me.

And then I tried to think about what I had to do, but I couldn't think because there were too many other things in my head, so I did a maths problem to make my head clearer.

And the maths problem that I did was called **Conway's Soldiers.** And in **Conway's Soldiers** you have a chessboard that continues infinitely in all directions and every square below a horizontal line has a colored tile on it like this

And you can move a colored tile only if it can jump over a colored tile horizontally or vertically (but not diagonally) into an

empty square 2 squares away. And when you move a colored tile in this way you have to remove the colored tile that it jumped over, like this

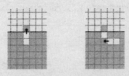

And you have to see how far you get the colored tiles above the starting horizontal line, and you start by doing something like this

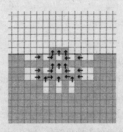

And then you do something like this

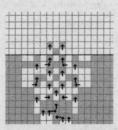

And I know what the answer is because however you move the colored tiles you will never get a colored tile more than 4 squares above the starting horizontal line, but it is a good maths

147

problem to do in your head when you don't want to think about something else because you can make it as complicated as you need to fill your brain by making the board as big as you want and the moves as complicated as you want.

And I had got to

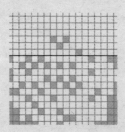

and then I looked up and saw that there was a policeman standing in front of me and he was saying, "Anyone at home?" but I didn't know what that meant.

And then he said, "Are you all right, young man?"

I looked at him and I thought for a bit so that I would answer the question correctly and I said, "No."

And he said, "You're looking a bit worse for wear."

He had a gold ring on one of his fingers and it had curly letters on it but I couldn't see what the letters were.

Then he said, "The lady at the café says you've been here for 2½ hours, and when she tried talking to you, you were in a complete trance."

Then he said, "What's your name?"

And I said, "Christopher Boone."

And he said, "Where do you live?"

And I said, "36 Randolph Street," and I started feeling better because I like policemen and it was an easy question, and I wondered whether I should tell him that Father killed Wellington and whether he would arrest Father.

And he said, "What are you doing here?"

And I said, "I needed to sit down and be quiet and think."

And he said, "OK, let's keep it simple. What are you doing at the railway station?"

And I said, "I'm going to see Mother."

And he said, "Mother?"

And I said, "Yes, Mother."

And he said, "When's your train?"

And I said, "I don't know. She lives in London. I don't know when there's a train to London."

And he said, "So, you don't live with your mother?"

And I said, "No. But I'm going to."

And then he sat down next to me and said, "So, where does your mother live?"

And I said, "In London."

And he said, "Yes, but where in London?"

And I said, "451c Chapter Road, London NW2 5NG."

And he said, "Jesus. What is that?"

And I looked down and I said, "That's my pet rat, Toby," because he was looking out of my pocket at the policeman.

And the policeman said, "A pet rat?"

And I said, "Yes, a pet rat. He's very clean and he hasn't got bubonic plague."

And the policeman said, "Well that's reassuring."

And I said, "Yes."

And he said, "Have you got a ticket?"

And I said, "No."

And he said, "Have you got any money to get a ticket?"

And I said, "No."

And he said, "So, how precisely were you going to get to London, then?"

And then I didn't know what to say because I had Father's cashpoint card in my pocket and it was illegal to steal things, but he was a policeman so I had to tell the truth, so I said, "I have a cashpoint card," and I took it out of my pocket and I showed it to him. And this was a white lie.

But the policeman said, "Is this your card?"

And then I thought he might arrest me, and I said, "No, it's Father's."

And he said, "Father's?"

And I said, "Yes, Father's."

And he said, "OK," but he said it really slowly and he squeezed his nose between his thumb and his forefinger.

And I said, "He told me the number," which was another white lie.

And he said, "Why don't you and I take a stroll to the cashpoint machine, eh?"

And I said, "You mustn't touch me."

And he said, "Why would I want to touch you?"

And I said, "I don't know."

And he said, "Well neither do I."

And I said, "Because I got a caution for hitting a policeman, but I didn't mean to hurt him and if I do it again I'll get into even bigger trouble."

Then he looked at me and he said, "You're serious, aren't you."

And I said, "Yes."

And he said, "You lead the way."

And I said, "Where?"

And he said, "Back by the ticket office," and he pointed with his thumb.

And then we walked back through the tunnel, but it wasn't so frightening this time because there was a policeman with me.

And I put the cashpoint card into the machine like Father had let me do sometimes when we were shopping together and it said **ENTER YOUR PERSONAL NUMBER** and I typed in **3558** and pressed the **ENTER** button and the machine said **PLEASE ENTER AMOUNT** and there was a choice

← £10   £20 →

← £50   £100 →

Other Amount

(multiples of ten only) →

And I asked the policeman, "How much does it cost to get a ticket for a train to London?"

And he said, "About 30 quid."

And I said, "Is that pounds?"

And he said, "Christ alive," and he laughed. But I didn't laugh because I don't like people laughing at me, even if they are policemen. And he stopped laughing, and he said, "Yep. It's 30 pounds."

So I pressed **£50** and five £10 notes came out of the machine, and a receipt, and I put the notes and the receipt and the card into my pocket.

And the policeman said, "Well, I guess I shouldn't keep you chatting any longer."

And I said, "Where do I get a ticket for the train from?" because if you are lost and you need directions you can ask a policeman.

And he said, "You are a prize specimen, aren't you."

And I said, "Where do I get a ticket for the train from?" because he hadn't answered my question.

And he said, "In there," and he pointed and there was a big room with a glass window on the other side of the train station door, and then he said, "Now, are you sure you know what you're doing?"

And I said, "Yes. I'm going to London to live with my mother."

And he said, "Has your mother got a telephone number?"

And I said, "Yes."

And he said, "And can you tell me what it is?"

And I said, "Yes. It's 0208 887 8907."

And he said, "And you'll ring her if you get into any trouble, OK?"

And I said, "Yes," because I knew you could ring people from phone boxes if you had money, and I had money now.

And he said, "Good."

And I walked into the ticket office and I turned round and I could see that the policeman was still watching me so I felt safe. And there was a long desk at the other side of the big room and a window on the desk and there was a man standing in front of the window and there was a man behind the window, and I said to the man behind the window, "I want to go to London."

And the man in front of the window said, "If you don't mind," and he turned round so that his back was toward me and the man behind the window gave him a little bit of paper to sign and he signed it and pushed it back under the window and the

152

man behind the window gave him a ticket. And then the man in front of the window looked at me and he said, "What the fuck are you looking at?" and then he walked away.

And he had dreadlocks, which is what some black people have, but he was white, and dreadlocks is when you never wash your hair and it looks like old rope. And he had red trousers with stars on them. And I kept my hand on my Swiss Army knife in case he touched me.

And then there was no one else in front of the window and I said to the man behind the window, "I want to go to London," and I hadn't been frightened when I was with the policeman but I turned round and I saw that he had gone now and I was scared again, so I tried to pretend I was playing a game on my computer and it was called **Train to London** and it was like **Myst** or **The 11th Hour,** and you had to solve lots of different problems to get to the next level, and I could turn it off at any time.

And the man said, "Single or return?"

And I said, "What does *single or return* mean?"

And he said, "Do you want to go one way, or do you want to go and come back?"

And I said, "I want to stay there when I get there."

And he said, "For how long?"

And I said, "Until I go to university."

And he said, "Single, then," and then he said, "That'll be £32."

And I gave him the fifty pounds and he gave me £10 back and he said, "Don't you go throwing it away."

And then he gave me a little yellow and orange ticket and £8 in coins and I put it all in my pocket with my knife. And I didn't like the ticket being half yellow but I had to keep it because it was my train ticket.

And then he said, "If you could move away from the counter."

And I said, "When is the train to London?"

And he looked at his watch and said, "Platform 1, five minutes."

And I said, "Where is Platform 1?"

And he pointed and said, "Through the underpass and up the stairs. You'll see the signs."

And *underpass* meant *tunnel* because I could see where he was pointing, so I went out of the ticket office, but it wasn't like a computer game at all because I was in the middle of it and it was like all the signs were shouting in my head and someone bumped into me as they walked past and I made a noise like a dog barking to scare them off.

And I pictured in my head a big red line across the floor which started at my feet and went through the tunnel and I started walking along the red line, saying, "Left, right, left, right, left, right," because sometimes when I am frightened or angry it helps if I do something that has a rhythm to it, like music or drumming, which is something Siobhan taught me to do.

And I went up the stairs and I saw a sign saying ← **Platform 1** and the ← was pointing at a glass door so I went through it, and someone bumped into me again with a suitcase and I made another noise like a dog barking, and they said, "Watch where the hell you're going," but I pretended that they were just one of the Guarding Demons in **Train to London** and there was a train. And I saw a man with a newspaper and a bag of golf clubs go up to one of the doors of the train and press a big button next to it and the doors were electronic and they slid open and I liked that. And then the doors closed behind him.

And then I looked at my watch and 3 minutes had gone

past since I was at the ticket office, which meant that the train would be going in 2 minutes.

And then I went up to the door and I pressed the big button and the doors slid open and I stepped through the doors.

And I was on the train to London.

193.   When I used to play with my train set I made a train timetable because I liked timetables. And I like timetables because I like to know when everything is going to happen.

And this was my timetable when I lived at home with Father and I thought that Mother was dead from a heart attack (this was the timetable for a Monday and also it is an *approximation*)

7:20 a.m.	Wake up	8:43 a.m.	Go past tropical fish shop
7:25 a.m.	Clean teeth and wash face	8:51 a.m.	Arrive at school
7:30 a.m.	Give Toby food and water	9:00 a.m.	School assembly
		9:15 a.m.	First morning class
7:40 a.m.	Have breakfast	10:30 a.m.	Break
8:00 a.m.	Put school clothes on	10:50 a.m.	Art class with Mrs. Peters[15]
8:05 a.m.	Pack schoolbag		
8:10 a.m.	Read book or watch video	12:30 p.m.	Lunch
		1:00 p.m.	First afternoon class
8:32 a.m.	Catch bus to school	2:15 p.m.	Second afternoon class

[15] In the art class we do art, but in the first morning class and the first afternoon class and the second afternoon class we do lots of different things like **Reading** and **Tests** and **Social Skills** and **Looking after Animals** and **What We Did at the Weekend** and **Writing** and **Maths** and **Stranger Danger** and **Money** and **Personal Hygiene.**

3:30 p.m.	Catch school bus home	6:00 p.m.	Have tea
3:49 p.m.	Get off school bus at home	6:30 p.m.	Watch television or a video
3:50 p.m.	Have juice and snack	7:00 p.m.	Do maths practice
3:55 p.m.	Give Toby food and water	8:00 p.m.	Have a bath
4:00 p.m.	Take Toby out of his cage	8:15 p.m.	Get changed into pajamas
4:18 p.m.	Put Toby into his cage	8:20 p.m.	Play computer games
4:20 p.m.	Watch television or video	9:00 p.m.	Watch television or a video
5:00 p.m.	Read a book	9:20 p.m.	Have juice and a snack
		9:30 p.m.	Go to bed

And at the weekend I make up my own timetable and I write it down on a piece of cardboard and I put it up on the wall. And it says things like **Feed Toby** or **Do maths** or **Go to the shop to buy sweets.** And that is one of the other reasons why I don't like France, because when people are on holiday they don't have a timetable and I had to get Mother and Father to tell me every morning exactly what we were going to do that day to make me feel better.

Because time is not like space. And when you put something down somewhere, like a protractor or a biscuit, you can have a map in your head to tell you where you have left it, but even if you don't have a map it will still be there because a map is a *representation* of things that actually exist so you can find the protractor or the biscuit again. And a timetable is a map of time, except that if you don't have a timetable time is not there like the landing and the garden and the route to school. Because time is only the relationship between the way different things change, like the earth going round the sun and atoms vibrating and clocks ticking and day and night and waking up and going to sleep, and it is like west or nor-nor-east, which won't exist when the earth stops existing and falls into the sun because it is only a relationship between the North Pole and the South Pole and everywhere else, like Mogadishu and Sunderland and Canberra.

And it isn't a fixed relationship like the relationship between our house and Mrs. Shears's house, or like the relationship between 7 and 865, but it depends on how fast you are going relative to a specific point. And if you go off in a spaceship and you travel near the speed of light, you may come back and find that all your family is dead and you are still young and it will be the future but your clock will say that you have only been away for a few days or months.

And because nothing can travel faster than the speed of light, this means that we can only know about a fraction of the things that go on in the universe, like this

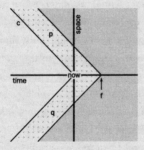

And this is a map of everything and everywhere, and the future is on the right and the past is on the left and the gradient of the line **c** is the speed of light, but we can't know about the things which happen in the shaded areas even though some of them have already happened, but when we get to **f** it will be possible to find out about things which happen in the lighter areas **p** and **q**.

And this means that time is a mystery, and not even a thing, and no one has ever solved the puzzle of what time is, exactly. And so, if you get lost in time it is like being lost in a desert, except that you can't see the desert because it is not a thing.

And this is why I like timetables, because they make sure you don't get lost in time.

197.   There were lots of people on the train, and I didn't like that, because I don't like lots of people I don't know and I hate it even more if I am stuck in a room with lots of people I don't know, and a train is like a room and you can't get out of it when it's moving. And it made me think of when I had to come home in the car from school one day because the bus had broken down and Mother came and picked me up and Mrs. Peters asked Mother if she could take Jack and Polly home because their mothers couldn't come and pick them up, and Mother said yes. But I started screaming in the car because there were too many people in it and Jack and Polly weren't in my class and Jack bangs his head on things and makes a noise like an animal, and I tried to get out of the car, but it was still going along and I fell out onto the road and I had to have stitches in my head and they had to shave the hair off and it took 3 months for it to grow back to the way it was before.

So I stood very still in the train carriage and didn't move.

And then I heard someone say "Christopher."

And I thought it would be someone I knew, like a teacher from school or one of the people who live in our street, but it wasn't. It was the policeman again. And he said, "Caught you just in time," and he was breathing really loud and holding his knees.

And I didn't say anything.

And he said, "We've got your father at the police station."

And I thought he was going to say that they had arrested Father for killing Wellington, but he didn't. He said, "He's looking for you."

And I said, "I know."

And he said, "So, why are you going to London?"

And I said, "Because I'm going to live with Mother."

And he said, "Well, I think your father might have something to say about that."

And then I thought that he was going to take me back to Father and that was frightening because he was a policeman and policemen are meant to be good, so I started to run away, but he grabbed me and I screamed. And then he let go.

And he said, "OK, let's not get overexcited here." And then he said, "I'm going to take you back to the police station and you and me and your dad can sit down and have a little chat about who's going where."

And I said, "I'm going to live with Mother, in London."

And he said, "Not just yet you're not."

And I said, "Have you arrested Father?"

And he said, "Arrested him? What for?"

And I said, "He killed a dog. With a garden fork. The dog was called Wellington."

And the policeman said, "Did he now?"

And I said, "Yes, he did."

And he said, "Well, we can talk about that as well." And then he said, "Right, young man, I think you've done enough adventuring for one day."

And then he reached out to touch me again and I started to scream again, and he said, "Now listen, you little monkey. You can either do what I say or I am going to have to make—"

And then the train jiggled and it began to move.

And then the policeman said, "Shitting fuck."

And then he looked at the ceiling of the train and he put his hands together in front of his mouth like people do when they are praying to God in heaven and he breathed really loudly into his hands and made a whistling noise, and then he stopped because the train jiggled again and he had to grab hold of one of the straps which were hanging from the ceiling.

And then he said, "Don't move."

And then he took out his walkie-talkie and pressed a button and said, "Rob . . . ? Yeah, it's Nigel. I'm stuck on the bloody train. Yeah. Don't even . . . Look. It stops at Didcot Parkway. So, if you can get someone to meet me with a car . . . Cheers. Tell his old man we've got him but it's going to take a while, OK? Great."

And then he clicked his walkie-talkie off and he said, "Let's get ourselves a seat," and he pointed to two long seats nearby which faced each other, and he said, "Park yourself. And no monkey business."

And the people who were sitting on the seats got up and walked away because he was a policeman and we sat down facing one another.

And he said, "You are a bloody handful, you are. Jeez."

And I wondered whether the policeman would help me find 451c Chapter Road, London NW2 5NG.

And I looked out of the window and we were going past factories and scrap yards full of old cars and there were 4 caravans in a muddy field with 2 dogs and some clothes hanging up to dry.

And outside the window was like a map, except that it was in 3 dimensions and it was life-size because it was the thing it was a map of. And there were so many things it made my head hurt, so I closed my eyes, but then I opened them again because it was like flying, but nearer to the ground, and I think flying is good. And then the countryside started and there were fields and cows and horses and a bridge and a farm and more houses and lots of little roads with cars on them. And that made me think that there must be millions of miles of train track in the world and they all go past houses and roads and rivers and fields, and that made me think how many people must be in the world and they all have houses and roads to travel on and cars and pets and clothes and they all eat lunch and go to bed and have names and this made my head hurt, too, so I closed my eyes again and did counting and groaning.

And when I opened my eyes the policeman was reading a newspaper called *The Sun,* and on the front of the paper it said **£3m Anderson's Call Girl Shame** and it had a picture of a man and a picture of a lady in a bra underneath.

And then I did some maths practice in my head, solving quadratic equations using the formula

$$x = \frac{-b \pm \sqrt{(b^2 - 4\,ac)}}{2a}$$

And then I wanted to go for a wee, but I was on a train. And I didn't know how long it would take us to get to London and I felt a panic starting, and I started to tap a rhythm on the glass with my knuckles to help me wait and not think about wanting to go for a wee, and I looked at my watch and I waited for 17 minutes, but when I want to go for a wee I have to go really quickly, which is why I like to be at home or at school and I always go for a wee before I get on the bus, which is why I leaked a bit and wet my trousers.

And then the policeman looked across at me and said, "Oh Christ, you've..." And then he put his newspaper down and said, "For God's sake go to the bloody toilet, will you."

And I said, "But I'm on a train."

And he said, "They do have toilets on trains, you know."

And I said, "Where is the toilet on the train?"

And he pointed and said, "Through those doors there. But I'll be keeping an eye on you, understand?"

And I said, "No," because I knew what *keeping an eye on someone* meant but he couldn't look at me when I was in the toilet.

And he said, "Just go to the bloody toilet."

So I got up out of my seat and I closed my eyes so that my eyelids were just little slits so I couldn't see the other people on the train and I walked to the door, and when I got through the door there was another door on the right and it was half open and it said **TOILET** on it, so I went inside.

And it was horrible inside because there was poo on the seat of the toilet and it smelled of poo, like the toilet at school when Joseph has been for a poo on his own, because he plays with it.

And I didn't want to use the toilet because of the poo, which was the poo of people I didn't know and brown, but I had to because I really wanted to wee. So I closed my eyes and went for a wee and the train wobbled and lots went on the seat and on the floor, but I wiped my penis with toilet paper and flushed the toilet and then I tried to use the sink but the tap didn't work, so I put spit on my hands and wiped them with a paper tissue and put it into the toilet.

Then I went out of the toilet and I saw that opposite the toilet there were two shelves with cases and a rucksack on them and it made me think of the airing cupboard at home and how I climb in there sometimes and it makes me feel safe. So I climbed onto the middle shelf and I pulled one of the cases across like a door so that I was shut in, and it was dark and there was no one in there with me and I couldn't hear people talking so I felt much calmer and it was nice.

And I did some more quadratic equations like

$$0 = 437x^2 + 103x + 11$$

and

$$0 = 79x^2 + 43x + 2089$$

and I made some of the coefficients large so that they were hard to solve.

And then the train started to slow down and someone came and stood near the shelf and knocked on the door of the toilet, and it was the policeman and he said, "Christopher . . . ? Christopher . . . ?" and then he opened the door of the toilet and said, "Bloody hell," and he was really close so that I could see his walkie-talkie and his truncheon on his belt and I could smell his aftershave, but he didn't see me and I didn't say anything because I didn't want him to take me to Father.

And then he went away again, running.

And then the train stopped and I wondered if it was London, but I didn't move because I didn't want the policeman to find me.

And then a lady with a jumper that had bees and flowers

made of wool on it came and took the rucksack off the shelf over my head and she said, "You scared the living daylights out of me."

But I didn't say anything.

And then she said, "I think someone's out there on the platform looking for you."

But I carried on not saying anything.

And she said, "Well, it's your lookout," and she went away.

And then 3 other people walked past and one of them was a black man in a long white dress and he put a big parcel on the shelf above my head but he didn't see me.

And then the train started going again.

199. People believe in God because the world is very complicated and they think it is very unlikely that anything as complicated as a flying squirrel or the human eye or a brain could happen by chance. But they should think logically and if they thought logically they would see that they can only ask this question because it has already happened and they exist. And there are billions of planets where there is no life, but there is no one on those planets with brains to notice. And it is like if everyone in the world was tossing coins eventually someone would get 5,698 heads in a row and they would think they were very special. But they wouldn't be because there would be millions of people who didn't get 5,698 heads.

And there is life on earth because of an accident. But it is a very special kind of accident. And for this accident to happen in this special way, there have to be 3 *conditions*. And these are

1. Things have to make copies of themselves (this is called **Replication**)

2. They have to make small mistakes when they do this (this is called **Mutation**)

3. These mistakes have to be the same in their copies (this is called **Heritability**)

And these conditions are very rare, but they are possible, and they cause life. And it just happens. But it doesn't have to end up with rhinoceroses and human beings and whales. It could end up with anything.

And, for example, some people say how can an eye happen by accident? Because an eye has to evolve from something else very like an eye and it doesn't just happen because of a genetic mistake, and what is the use of half an eye? But half an eye is very useful because half an eye means that an animal can see half of an animal that wants to eat it and get out of the way, and it will eat the animal that only has a third of an eye or 49% of an eye instead because it hasn't got out of the way quick enough, and the animal that is eaten won't have babies because it is dead. And 1% of an eye is better than no eye.

And people who believe in God think God has put human beings on the earth because they think human beings are the best animal, but human beings are just an animal and they will evolve into another animal, and that animal will be cleverer and it will put human beings into a zoo, like we put chimpanzees and gorillas into a zoo. Or human beings will all catch a disease and die out or they will make too much pollution and kill themselves, and then there will only be insects in the world and they will be the best animal.

211.   Then I wondered whether I should have got off the train because it had just stopped at London, and I was scared because if the train went anywhere else it would be somewhere where I didn't know anybody.

And then somebody went to the toilet and then they came out again, but they didn't see me. And I could smell their poo, and it was different from the smell of the poo that I smelled in the toilet when I went in there.

And then I closed my eyes and did some more maths puzzles so I didn't think about where I was going.

And then the train stopped again, and I thought about getting off the shelf and going to get my bag and get off the train. But I didn't want to be found by the policeman and be taken to Father, so I stayed on the shelf and didn't move, and no one saw me this time.

And then I remembered that there was a map on the wall of one of the classrooms at school, and it was a map of England and Scotland and Wales and it showed you where all the towns were and I pictured it in my head with Swindon and London on it, and it was like this in my head

And I had been looking at my watch since the train had started at **12:59 p.m.** And the first stop had been at **1:16 p.m.**, which was 17 minutes later. And it was now **1:39 p.m.**, which

was 23 minutes after the stop, which meant that we would be at the sea if the train didn't go in a big curve. But I didn't know if it went in a big curve.

And then there were another 4 stops and 4 people came and took bags away from the shelves and 2 people put bags on the shelves, but no one moved the big suitcase that was in front of me and only one person saw me and they said, "You are fucking weird, mate," and that was a man in a suit. And 6 people went to the toilet but they didn't do poos that I could smell, which was good.

And then the train stopped and a lady with a yellow waterproof coat came and took the big suitcase away and she said, "Have you touched this?"

And I said, "Yes."

And then she went away.

And then a man stood next to the shelf and said, "Come and look at this, Barry. They've got, like, a train elf."

And another man came and stood next to him and said, "Well, we have both been drinking."

And the first man said, "Perhaps we should feed him some nuts."

And the second man said, "You're the one who's bloody nuts."

And the first one said, "Come on, shift it, you daft cunt. I need more beers before I sober up."

And then they went away.

And then the train was really quiet and it didn't move again and I couldn't hear anyone. So I decided to get off the shelf and go and get my bag and see if the policeman was still sitting in his seat.

So I got off the shelf and I looked through the door, but the policeman wasn't there. And my bag had gone as well, which had Toby's food in it and my maths books and my clean pants and vest and shirt and the orange juice and the milk and the custard creams and the baked beans.

And then I heard the sound of feet and I turned round and it was another policeman, not the one who was on the train before, and I could see him through the door, in the next carriage, and he was looking under the seats. And I decided that I didn't like policemen so much anymore, so I got off the train.

And when I saw how big the room was that the train was in and I heard how noisy and echoey it was, I had to kneel down on the ground for a bit because I thought I was going to fall over. And when I was kneeling on the ground I worked out which way to walk, and I decided to walk in the direction the train was going when it came into the station because if this was the last stop, that was the direction London was in.

So I stood up and I imagined that there was a big red line on the ground which ran parallel to the train to the gate at the far end and I walked along it and I said, "Left, right, left, right . . ." again, like before.

And when I got to the gate a man said to me, "I think someone's looking for you, sonny."

And I said, "Who's looking for me?" because I thought it might be Mother and the policeman in Swindon had phoned her up with the phone number I told him.

But he said, "A policeman."

And I said, "I know."

And he said, "Oh. Right." And then he said, "You wait here, then, and I'll go and tell them," and he walked back down the side of the train.

So I carried on walking. And I could still feel the feeling like a balloon inside my chest and it hurt and I covered my ears with my hands and I went and stood against the wall of a little shop which said **Hotel and Theatre Reservations Tel: 0207 402 5164** in the middle of the big room and then I took my hands away from my ears and I groaned to block out the noise and I looked round the big room at all the signs to see if this was London. And the signs said

Sweet Pastries **Heathrow Airport Check-In Here** *Bagel Factory* **EAT**

excellence and taste YO! sushi **Stationlink** Buses **W H Smith**

Mezzanine **Heathrow Express Clinique First Class Lounge**

FULLERS easyCar.com *The Mad Bishop* **and Bear Public House**

Fuller's London Pride Dixons Our Price Paddington Bear at

Paddington Station Tickets Taxis ♦ ♦ **Toilets** First Aid **Eastbourne**

Terrace ▬▬▬▬▬**ington Way Out Praed Street The Lawn Q Here**

Please Upper Crust Sainsbury's Local ⓘ**Information** Great

Western First ℗ **Position Closed Position Closed Position**

Closed Sock Shop Fast Ticket Point ☺ **Millie's Cookies Coffee**

AIRLINERS COLLIDE OVER INDONESIA: 350 FEARED DEAD

Freshly Baked Cookies and Muffins Cold Drinks Penalty Fares

Warning Savoury Pastries Platforms 9-14 Burger King Fresh

Filled! the reef° café bar **business travel special edition TOP 75**

ALBUMS Evening Standard

But after a few seconds they looked like this

Sweathr⚡⚡◼ow◍℃Airpheck**lagtory**EAenceandtaste𝐘𝐎!suusetHee

sortCWHSmithEANEINStatᴅʜ✳ioe*ad*BhoathrnieFirlassLoULERnreHe

BSeasyCar.com*TheMp*anardBeʙʟᴇFuʟʟer'sLonPrᵃᵈᵃidePaiesstrDzzix

onsOur*is*PPurdEboi▨⏃aceicHousPatCngtoneawatPoagtonTetsTa*el*

Fac✝ToileddistsFirs⟜◉ta⚖B^{ung}feFi5us✖★HPDNLeTerrace◼◼◼

◼ingtonW✜astaySt◗atio✎◼nlinkOutC◼osed?&qed3iniBr1uow

o[CliPraicxis*k*eIDdPointDrS◼treetTheLyuawHea⊘◼rCrustMufly

B▨akl6dE✝TonClose"♦excelle^{toxpr}essnQinrePlek4shSaisesUp①

←⋏pensburiy'sᴸcidSo◼◼T◌◼◼◼◼◼**ation**REATM✚✚ASTERCoINEokie

sWᴇsᴛEfinsCojRN2FningSTan①◎RST℗P0allnforositioNCH✕⊕❌E

nSTAYATS3hopFast◎ʀ◎Positd◻Penie⤳⚡sPloNIa8⑨◼④⊃◆tfoe9

sWef°cusCoffReosᴠeledPOSI◻tnesskix①edcoreshoj◉✕③☐5ALBial

edᴍᴍᵢiafébarbeeanCrKl'geing◐F3illeFFTOUr⚡mEGIEs9TEDFrese

✳◻◻sanaltyFarmingSa◉vou^{ryPa}stri14Burzd!the◗◼•resit✳◻rh▤◻

aspecitionTOP7UMSEvedard

because there were too many and my brain wasn't working properly and this frightened me so I closed my eyes again and I counted slowly to 50 but without doing the cubes. And I stood there and I opened my Swiss Army knife in my pocket to make me feel safe and I held on to it tight.

And then I made my hand into a little tube with my fingers and I opened my eyes and I looked through the tube so that I was only looking at one sign at a time and after a long time I saw a sign that said ①**Information** and it was above a window on a little shop.

And a man came up to me and he was wearing a blue jacket and blue trousers and he had brown shoes and he was carrying a book in his hand and he said, "You look lost."

So I took out my Swiss Army knife.

And he said, "Whoa. Whoa. Whoa. Whoa. Whoa," and held up both his hands with his fingers stretched out in a fan, like he wanted me to stretch my fingers out in a fan and touch his fingers because he wanted to say he loved me, but he did it with both hands, not one like Father and Mother, and I didn't know who he was.

And then he walked away backward.

So I went to the shop that said ①**Information** and I could feel my heart beating very hard and I could hear a noise like the sea in my ears. And when I got to the window I said, "Is this London?" but there was no one behind the window.

And then someone sat behind the window and she was a lady and she was black and she had long fingernails which were painted pink and I said, "Is this London?"

And she said, "Sure is, honey."

And I said, "Is this London?"

And she said, "Indeed it is."

And I said, "How do I get to 451c Chapter Road, London NW2 5NG?"

And she said, "Where is that?"

And I said, "It's 451c Chapter Road, London NW2 5NG. And sometimes you can write it *451c Chapter Road, Willesden, London NW2 5NG.*"

And the lady said to me, "Take the tube to Willesden Junction, honey. Or Willesden Green. Got to be near there some-where."

And I said, "What sort of tube?"

And she said, "Are you for real?"

And I didn't say anything.

And she said, "Over there. See that big staircase with the escalators? See the sign? Says *Underground*. Take the Bakerloo Line to Willesden Junction or the Jubilee to Willesden Green. You OK, honey?"

And I looked where she was pointing and there was a big staircase going down into the ground and there was a big sign over the top of it like this

And I thought, "I can do this," because I was doing really well and I was in London and I would find my mother. And I had to think to myself, "The people are like cows in a field," and I just had to look in front of me all the time and make a red line along the floor in the picture of the big room in my head and follow it.

And I walked across the big room to the escalators. And I kept hold of my Swiss Army knife in my pocket and I held on to Toby in my other pocket to make sure he didn't escape.

And *the escalators* was a staircase but it was moving and people stepped onto it and it carried them down and up and it made me laugh because I hadn't been on one before and it was like something in a science fiction film about the future. But I didn't want to use it so I went down the stairs instead.

And then I was in a smaller room underground and there were lots of people and there were pillars which had blue lights in the ground around the bottom of them and I liked these but I didn't like the people, so I saw a photo booth like one I went into on 25 March 1994 to have my passport photo done, and I went into the photo booth because it was like a cupboard and it felt safer and I could look out through the curtain.

And I did detecting by watching and I saw that people were putting tickets into gray gates and walking through. And some of them were buying tickets at big black machines on the wall.

And I watched 47 people do this and I memorized what to do. Then I imagined a red line on the floor and I walked over to the wall where there was a poster which was a list of places to go and it was alphabetical and I saw **Willesden Green** and it said **£2:20** and then I went to one of the machines and there was a little screen which said **PRESS TICKET TYPE** and I pressed the button that most people had pressed, which was **ADULT SINGLE** and **£2:20,** and the screen said **INSERT £2:20** and I put three £1 coins into the slot and there was a clinking noise and the screen said **TAKE TICKET AND CHANGE** and there was a ticket in a little hole at the bottom of the machine and a 50p coin and a 20p coin and a 10p coin and I put the coins in my pocket and I went up to one of the gray gates and I put my ticket into the slot and it sucked it in and it came out on the other side of the gate. And someone said, "Get a move on," and I made the noise like a dog barking and I walked forward and the gate opened this time and I took my ticket like other people did and I liked the gray gate because that was like something in a science fiction film about the future, too.

And then I had to work out which way to go, so I stood

against a wall so people didn't touch me, and there was a sign for **Bakerloo Line** and **District and Circle Line** but not one for **Jubilee Line** like the lady had said, so I made a plan and it was *to go to Willesden Junction on the Bakerloo Line.*

And there was another sign for **Bakerloo Line** and it was like this

And I read all the words and I found **Willesden Junction,** so I followed the arrow that said ← and I went through the left-hand tunnel and there was a fence down the middle of the tunnel and the people were walking straight ahead on the left and coming the other way on the right like on a road, so I walked along the left and the tunnel curved left and then there were more gates and a sign said **Bakerloo Line** and it pointed down an escalator, so I had to go down the escalators and I had to hold on to the rubber rail but that moved too so I didn't fall over and people were standing close to me and I wanted to hit them to make them go away but I didn't hit them because of the caution.

And then I was at the bottom of the escalators and I had to jump off and I tripped and bumped into someone and they said, "Easy," and there were two ways to go and one said **Northbound** and I went that way because **Willesden** was on the top half of the map and the top is always north on maps.

And then I was in another train station but it was tiny and it was in a tunnel and there was only one track and the walls were curved and they were covered in big adverts and they said **WAY OUT** and **London's Transport Museum** and **Take time out to regret your career choice** and **JAMAICA** and **≓ British Rail** and **☻ No Smoking** and **Be Moved** and **Be Moved** and **Be Moved** and **For Stations beyond Queen's Park take the first train and change at Queen's Park if necessary** and **Hammersmith and City Line** and **You're closer than my family ever gets.** And there were lots of people standing in the little station and it was underground so there weren't any windows and I didn't like that, so I found a seat which was a bench and I sat at the end of the bench.

And then lots of people started coming into the little station. And someone sat down on the other end of the bench and it was a lady who had a black briefcase and purple shoes and a brooch shaped like a parrot. And the people kept coming into the little station so that it was even more crowded than the big station. And then I couldn't see the walls anymore and the back of someone's jacket touched my knee and I felt sick and I started groaning really loudly and the lady on the bench stood up and no one else sat down. And I felt like I felt like when I had flu and I had to stay in bed all day and all of me hurt and I couldn't walk or eat or go to sleep or do maths.

And then there was a sound like people fighting with swords and I could feel a strong wind and a roaring started and I closed my eyes and the roaring got louder and I groaned really loudly but I couldn't block it out of my ears and I thought the little station was going to collapse or there was a big fire somewhere and I was going to die. And then the roaring turned into a clattering and a squealing and it got slowly quieter and then it stopped and I kept my eyes closed because I felt safer not seeing what was happening. And then I could hear people moving again because it was quieter. And I opened my eyes but I couldn't see anything at first because there were too many people. And then I saw that they were getting onto a train that wasn't there before and it was the train which was the roaring. And there was sweat running down my face from under my hair and I was moaning, not groaning, but different, like a dog when it has hurt its paw, and I heard the sound but I didn't realize it was me at first.

And then the train doors closed and the train started moving and it roared again but not as loud this time and 5 carriages went past and it went into the tunnel at the end of the little station and it was quiet again and the people were all walking into the tunnels that went out of the little station.

And I was shaking and I wanted to be back at home, and then I realized I couldn't be at home because Father was there and he told a lie and he killed Wellington, which meant that it wasn't my home anymore, my home was 451c Chapter Road, London NW2 5NG, and it scared me, having a wrong thought like, "I wish I was back at home again," because it meant my mind wasn't working properly.

And then more people came into the little station and it became fuller and then the roaring began again and I closed my eyes and I sweated and felt sick and I felt the feeling like a balloon inside my chest and it was so big I found it hard to breathe. And then the people went away on the train and the little station was empty again. And then it filled up with people and another train came with the same roaring. And it was exactly like having flu that time because I wanted it to stop, like you can just pull the plug of a computer out of the wall if it crashes, because I wanted to go to sleep so that I wouldn't have to think because the only thing I could think was how much it hurt because there was no room for anything else in my head, but I couldn't go to sleep and I just had to sit there and there was nothing to do except to wait and to hurt.

2 2 3 . And this is another description because Siobhan said I should do descriptions and it is a description of the advert that was on the wall of the little train station opposite me, but I can't remember all of it because I thought I was going to die.

And the advert said

DREAM HOLIDAY,

THINK KUONI

IN MALAYSIA

and behind the writing there was a big photograph of 2 orangutans and they were swinging on branches and there were trees behind them but the leaves were blurred because the camera was focusing on the orangutans and not the leaves and the orangutans were moving.

And *orangutan* comes from the Malaysian word **ōrang-hūtan,** which means *man of the woods,* but **ōranghūtan** isn't Malaysian for *orangutan.*

And adverts are pictures or television programs to make you buy things like cars or Snickers or use an Internet Service Provider. But this was an advert to make you go to Malaysia on a holiday. And Malaysia is in Southeast Asia and it is made up of peninsular Malaysia and Sabah and Sarawak and Labuan and the capital is Kuala Lumpur and the highest mountain is Mount Kinabalu, which is 4,101 meters high, but that wasn't on the advert.

And Siobhan says people go on holidays to see new things and relax, but it wouldn't make me relaxed and you can see new things by looking at earth under a microscope or drawing the shape of the solid made when 3 circular rods of equal thickness intersect at right angles. And I think that there are so many things just in one house that it would take years to think about all of them properly. And also, a thing is interesting because of thinking about it and not because of being new. For example, Siobhan showed me that you can wet your finger and rub the edge of a thin glass and make a singing noise. And you can put different amounts of water in different glasses and they make different notes because they have what are called different *resonant frequencies,* and you can play a tune like **Three Blind Mice.** And lots of people have thin glasses in their houses and they don't know you can do this.

And the advert said

Malaysia, truly Asia.

Stimulated by the sights and smells, you realise that you have arrived in a land of contrasts. You seek out the traditional, the natural and the cosmopolitan. Your memories stretch from city days to nature reserves to lazy hours on the beach. Prices from £575 per person.

Call us on 01306 747000, see your travel agent or visit the world at www.kuoni.co.uk.

A world of difference.

And there were three other pictures, and they were very small, and they were a palace and a beach and a palace.

And this is what the orangutans looked like

227. And I kept my eyes closed and I didn't look at my watch at all. And the trains coming in and out of the station were in a rhythm, like music or drumming. And it was like counting and saying, "Left, right, left, right, left, right . . ." which Siobhan taught me to do to make myself calm. And I was saying in my head, "Train coming. Train stopped. Train going. Silence. Train coming. Train stopped. Train going . . ." as if the trains were only in my mind. And normally I don't imagine things that aren't happening because it is a lie and it makes me feel scared, but it was better than watching the trains coming in and out of the station because that made me feel even more scared.

And I didn't open my eyes and I didn't look at my watch. And it was like being in a dark room with the curtains closed so I couldn't see anything, like when you wake up at night and the only sounds you hear are the sounds inside your head. And that made it better because it was like the little station wasn't there, outside my head, but I was in bed and I was safe.

And then the silences between the trains coming and going got longer and longer. And I could hear that there were fewer people in the little station when the train wasn't there, so I opened my eyes and I looked at my watch and it said 8:07 p.m. and I had been sitting on the bench for approximately 5 hours but it hadn't seemed like approximately 5 hours, except that my bottom hurt and I was hungry and thirsty.

And then I realized that Toby was missing because he was not in my pocket, and I didn't want him to be missing because we weren't in Father's house or Mother's house and there wasn't anyone to feed him in the little station and he would die and he might get run over by a train.

And then I looked up at the ceiling and I saw that there was a long black box which was a sign and it said

| 1 HARROW & WEALDSTONE | 2 MIN |
| 3 QUEEN'S PARK | 7 MIN |

And then the bottom line scrolled up and disappeared and a different line scrolled up into its place and the sign said

```
┌──────────────────────────────────────────┐
│  1  HARROW  &  WEALDSTONE  1  MIN          │
│  2  WILLESDEN  JUNCTION      4  MIN        │
└──────────────────────────────────────────┘
```

And then it changed again and it said

```
┌──────────────────────────────────────────┐
│     1  HARROW  &  WEALDSTONE               │
│ ◇◇ STAND BACK TRAIN APPROACHING ◇◇         │
└──────────────────────────────────────────┘
```

And then I heard the sound like sword fighting and the roaring of a train coming into the station and I worked out that there was a big computer somewhere and it knew where all the trains were and it sent messages to the black boxes in the little stations to say when the trains were coming, and that made me feel better because everything had an order and a plan.

And the train came into the little station and it stopped and 5 people got onto the train and another person ran into the little station and got on, and 7 people got off the train and then the doors closed automatically and the train went away. And when the next train came I wasn't so scared anymore because the sign said TRAIN APPROACHING so I knew it was going to happen.

And then I decided that I would look for Toby because there were only 3 people in the little station. So I stood up and I looked up and down the little station and in the doorways that went into tunnels but I couldn't see him anywhere. And then I looked down into the black lower-down bit where the rails were.

And then I saw two mice and they were black because they were covered in dirt. And I liked that because I like mice and rats. But they weren't Toby, so I carried on looking.

And then I saw Toby, and he was also in the lower-down bit where the rails were, and I knew he was Toby because he was white and he had a brown egg shape on his back. So I climbed down off the concrete. And he was eating a bit of rubbish that was an old sweet paper. And someone shouted, "Jesus. What are you doing?"

And I bent down to catch Toby but he ran off. And I walked after him and I bent down again and I said, "Toby . . . Toby . . . Toby," and I held out my hand so that he could smell my hand and smell that it was me.

And someone said, "Get out of there, for fuck's sake," and I looked up and it was a man who was wearing a green raincoat and he had black shoes and his socks were showing and they were gray with little diamond patterns on them.

And I said, "Toby . . . Toby . . ." but he ran off again.

And the man with the diamond patterns on his socks tried to grab my shoulder, so I screamed. And then I heard the sound like sword fighting and Toby started running again, but this time he ran the other way, which was past my feet, and I grabbed at him and I caught him by the tail.

And the man with the diamond patterns on his socks said, "Oh Christ. Oh Christ."

And then I heard the roaring and I lifted Toby up and grabbed him with both hands and he bit me on my thumb and there was blood coming out and I shouted and Toby tried to jump out of my hands.

And then the roaring got louder and I turned round and I saw the train coming out of the tunnel and I was going to be run over and killed so I tried to climb up onto the concrete but it was high and I was holding Toby in both my hands.

And then the man with the diamond patterns on his socks grabbed hold of me and pulled me and I screamed, but he kept pulling me and he pulled me up onto the concrete and we fell over and I carried on screaming because he had hurt my shoulder. And then the train came into the station and I stood up and I ran to the bench again and I put Toby into the pocket inside my jacket and he went very quiet and he didn't move.

And the man with the diamond patterns on his socks was standing next to me and he said, "What the fuck do you think you were playing at?"

But I didn't say anything.

And he said, "What were you doing?"

And the doors of the train opened and people got off and there was a lady standing behind the man with the diamond patterns on his socks and she was carrying a guitar case like Siobhan has.

And I said, "I was finding Toby. He's my pet rat."

And the man with the diamond patterns on his socks said, "Fucking Nora."

And the lady with the guitar case said, "Is he OK?"

And the man with the diamond patterns on his socks said, "Him? Thanks a fucking bundle. Jesus Christ. A pet rat. Oh shit. My train." And then he ran to the train and he banged on the door, which was closed, and the train started to go away and he said, "Fuck."

And the lady said, "Are you OK?" and she touched my arm so I screamed again.

And she said, "OK. OK. OK."

And there was a sticker on her guitar case and it said

howl

records

And I was sitting on the ground and the woman knelt down on one knee and she said, "Is there anything I can do to help you?"

And if she was a teacher at school I could have said, "Where is 451c Chapter Road, Willesden, London NW2 5NG?" but she was a stranger, so I said, "Stand further away," because I didn't like her being so close. And I said, "I've got a Swiss Army knife and it has a saw blade and it could cut someone's fingers off."

And she said, "OK, buddy. I'm going to take that as a no," and she stood up and walked away.

And the man with the diamond patterns on his socks said, "Mad as a fucking hatter. Jesus," and he was pressing a handkerchief against his face and there was blood on the handkerchief.

And then another train came and the man with the diamond patterns on his socks and the lady with the guitar case got on and it went away again.

And then 8 more trains came and I decided that I would get onto a train and then I would work out what to do.

So I got on the next train.

And Toby tried to get out of my pocket so I took hold of him and I put him in my outside pocket and I held him with my hand.

And there were 11 people in the carriage and I didn't like

being in a room with 11 people in a tunnel, so I concentrated on things in the carriage. And there were signs saying **There are 53,963 holiday cottages in Scandinavia and Germany** and **VITABIOTICS** and **3435** and **Penalty £10 if you fail to show a valid ticket for your entire journey** and **Discover Gold, Then Bronze** and **TVIC** and **EPBIC** and **suck my cock** and ⚠ **Obstructing the doors can be dangerous** and **BRV** and **Con. IC** and **TALK TO THE WORLD.**

And there was a pattern on the walls which was like this

And there was a pattern on the seats like this

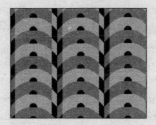

Then the train wobbled a lot and I had to hang on to a rail and we went into a tunnel and it was noisy and I closed my eyes and I could feel the blood pumping in the sides of my neck.

And then we came out of the tunnel and went into another little station and it was called **Warwick Avenue** and it said it in big letters on the wall and I liked that because you knew where you were.

And I timed the distance between stations all the way to

Willesden Junction and all the times between stations were multiples of 15 seconds like this

Paddington	0:00
Warwick Avenue	1:30
Maida Vale	3:15
Kilburn Park	5:00
Queen's Park	7:00
Kensal Green	10:30
Willesden Junction	11:45

And when the train stopped at **Willesden Junction** and the
doors opened automatically I walked out of the train. And then
the doors closed and the train went away. And everyone who got
off the train walked up a staircase and over a bridge except me.
and then there were only 2 people that I could see and one was
a man and he was drunk and he had brown stains on his coat and
his shoes were not a pair and he was singing but I couldn't hear
what he was singing, and the other was an Indian man in a shop
which was a little window in a wall.

And I didn't want to talk to either of them because I was
tired and hungry and I had already talked to lots of strangers.
which is dangerous, and the more you do something dangerous
the more likely it is that something bad happens. But I didn't
know how to get to 451c Chapter Road, London NW2 5NG, so I
had to ask somebody.

So I went up to the man in the little shop and I said.
"Where is 451c Chapter Road, London NW2 5NG?"

And he picked up a little book and handed it to me and
said, "Two ninety-five."

And the book was called *LONDON AZ Street Atlas and*

Index, Geographers' A–Z Map Company, and I opened it up and it was lots of maps.

And the man in the little shop said, "Are you going to buy it or not?"

And I said, "I don't know."

And he said, "Well, you can get your dirty fingers off it if you don't mind," and he took it back from me.

And I said, "Where is 451c Chapter Road, London NW2 5NG?"

And he said, "You can either buy the A-to-Z or you can hop it. I'm not a walking encyclopedia."

And I said, "Is that the A-to-Z?" and I pointed at the book.

And he said, "No, it's a sodding crocodile."

And I said, "Is that the A-to-Z?" because it wasn't a crocodile and I thought I had heard wrong because of his accent.

And he said, "Yes, it's the A-to-Z."

And I said, "Can I buy it?"

And he didn't say anything.

And I said, "Can I buy it?"

And he said, "Two pounds ninety-five, but you're giving me the money first. I'm not having you scarpering," and then I realized that he meant £2.95 when he said *Two ninety-five.*

And I paid him with my money and he gave me change just like in the shop at home and I went and sat down on the floor against the wall like the man with the dirty clothes but a long way away from him and I opened up the book.

And inside the front cover there was a big map of London with places on it like **Abbey Wood** and **Poplar** and **Acton** and **Stanmore.** And it said KEY TO MAP PAGES. And the map was covered with a grid and each square of the grid had two numbers on it. And **Willesden** was in the square which said **42** and **43**. And I worked out that the numbers were the numbers of the pages where you could see a bigger-scale map of that square of London. And the whole book was a big map of London, but it had been chopped up so it could be made into a book, and I liked that.

But Willesden Junction wasn't on pages 42 and 43. And I found it on page 58, which was directly under page 42 on the **KEY TO MAP PAGES** and which joined up with page 42. And I looked round Willesden Junction in a spiral, like when I was looking for the train station in Swindon, but on the map with my finger.

And the man who had shoes that did not match stood in front of me and said, "Big cheese. Oh yes. The nurses. Never. Bloody liar. Total bloody liar."

Then he went away.

And it took me a long time to find Chapter Road because it wasn't on page 58. It was back on page 42, and it was in square 5C.

And this was the shape of the roads between Willesden Junction and Chapter Road.

And this was my route

So I went up the staircase and over the bridge and I put my ticket in the little gray gate and went into the street and there was a bus and a big machine with a sign on it which said **English Welsh and Scottish Railways,** but it was yellow, and I looked around and it was dark and there were lots of bright lights and I hadn't been outside for a long time and it made me feel sick. And I kept my eyelids very close together and I just looked at the shape of the roads and then I knew which roads were **Station Approach** and **Oak Lane,** which were the roads I had to go along.

So I started walking, but Siobhan said I didn't have to describe everything that happens, I just have to describe the things that were interesting.

So I got to 451c Chapter Road, London NW2 5NG, and it took me 27 minutes and there was no one in when I pressed the button that said **Flat C** and the only interesting thing that happened on the way was 8 men dressed up in Viking costumes with helmets with horns on and they were shouting, but they weren't real Vikings because the Vikings lived nearly 2,000 years ago, and also I had to go for another wee and I went in the alleyway down the side of a garage called **Burdett Motors,** which was closed, and I didn't like doing that but I didn't want to wet myself again, and there was nothing else interesting.

So I decided to wait and I hoped that Mother was not on holiday because that would mean she could be away for more than a whole week, but I tried not to think about this because I couldn't go back to Swindon.

So I sat down on the ground behind the dustbins in the little garden that was in front of 451c Chapter Road, London NW2 5NG, and it was under a big bush. And a lady came into the garden and she was carrying a little box with a metal grille on one end and a handle on the top like you use to take a cat to the vet, but I couldn't see if there was a cat in it, and she had shoes with high heels and she didn't see me.

And then it started to rain and I got wet and I started shivering because I was cold.

And then it was 11:32 p.m. and I heard voices of people walking along the street.

And a voice said, "I don't care whether you thought it was funny or not," and it was a lady's voice.

And another voice said, "Judy, look. I'm sorry, OK," and it was a man's voice.

And the other voice, which was the lady's voice, said, "Well, perhaps you should have thought about that before you made me look like a complete idiot."

And the lady's voice was Mother's voice.

And Mother came into the garden and Mr. Shears was with her, and the other voice was his.

So I stood up and I said, "You weren't in, so I waited for you."

And Mother said, "Christopher."

And Mr. Shears said, "What?"

And Mother put her arms around me and said, "Christopher, Christopher, Christopher."

And I pushed her away because she was grabbing me and I didn't like it, and I pushed really hard and I fell over.

And Mr. Shears said, "What the hell is going on?"

And Mother said, "I'm so sorry, Christopher. I forgot."

And I was lying on the ground and Mother held up her right hand and spread her fingers out in a fan so that I could touch her fingers, but then I saw that Toby had escaped out of my pockets so I had to catch him.

And Mr. Shears said, "I suppose this means Ed's here."

And there was a wall around the garden so Toby couldn't get out because he was stuck in the corner and he couldn't climb up the walls fast enough and I grabbed him and put him back in my pocket and I said, "He's hungry. Have you got any food I can give him, and some water?"

And Mother said, "Where's your father, Christopher?"

And I said, "I think he's in Swindon."

And Mr. Shears said, "Thank God for that."

And Mother said, "But how did you get here?"

And my teeth were clicking against each other because of the cold and I couldn't stop them, and I said, "I came on the train. And it was really frightening. And I took Father's cashpoint card so I could get money out and a policeman helped me. But then he wanted to take me back to Father. And he was on the train with me. But then he wasn't."

And Mother said, "Christopher, you're soaking. Roger, don't just stand there."

And then she said, "Oh my God. Christopher. I didn't . . . I didn't think I'd ever . . . Why are you here on your own?"

And Mr. Shears said, "Are you going to come in or are you going to stay out here all night?"

And I said, "I'm going to live with you because Father killed Wellington with a garden fork and I'm frightened of him."

And Mr. Shears said, "Jumping Jack Christ."

And Mother said, "Roger, please. Come on, Christopher, let's go inside and get you dried off."

So I stood up and I went inside the house and Mother said, "You follow Roger," and I followed Mr. Shears up the stairs and there was a landing and a door which said **Flat C** and I was scared of going inside because I didn't know what was inside.

And Mother said, "Go on or you'll catch your death," but I didn't know what *you'll catch your death* meant, and I went inside.

And then she said, "I'll run you a bath," and I walked round the flat to make a map of it in my head so I felt safer, and the flat was like this

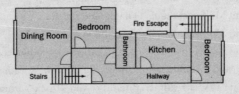

And then Mother made me take my clothes off and get into the bath and she said I could use her towel, which was purple with green flowers on the end. And she gave Toby a saucer of water and some bran flakes and I let him run around the bathroom. And he did three little poos under the sink and I picked them up and flushed them down the toilet and then I got back into the bath again because it was warm and nice.

Then Mother came into the bathroom and she sat on the toilet and she said, "Are you OK, Christopher?"

And I said, "I'm very tired."

And she said, "I know, love." And then she said, "You're very brave."

And I said, "Yes."

And she said, "You never wrote to me."

And I said, "I know."

And she said, "Why didn't you write to me, Christopher? I wrote you all those letters. I kept thinking something dreadful had happened, or you'd moved away and I'd never find out where you were."

And I said, "Father said you were dead."

And she said, "What?"

And I said, "He said you went into hospital because you had something wrong with your heart. And then you had a heart attack and died and he kept all the letters in a shirt box in the cupboard in his bedroom and I found them because I was looking for a book I was writing about Wellington being killed and he'd taken it away from me and hidden it in the shirt box."

And then Mother said, "Oh my God."

And then she didn't say anything for a long while. And then she made a loud wailing noise like an animal on a nature program on television.

And I didn't like her doing this because it was a loud noise, and I said, "Why are you doing that?"

And she didn't say anything for while, and then she said, "Oh, Christopher, I'm so sorry."

And I said, "It's not your fault."

And then she said, "Bastard. The bastard."

And then, after a while, she said, "Christopher, let me hold your hand. Just for once. Just for me. Will you? I won't hold it hard," and she held out her hand.

And I said, "I don't like people holding my hand."

And she took her hand back and she said, "No. OK. That's OK."

And then she said, "Let's get you out of the bath and dried off, OK?"

And I got out of the bath and dried myself with the purple towel. But I didn't have any pajamas so I put on a white T-shirt and a pair of yellow shorts which were Mother's, but I didn't mind because I was so tired. And while I was doing this Mother went into the kitchen and heated up some tomato soup because it was red.

And then I heard someone opening the door of the flat and there was a strange man's voice outside, so I locked the bathroom door. And there was an argument outside and a man said, "I need to speak to him," and Mother said, "He's been through enough today already," and the man said, "I know. But I still need to speak to him."

And Mother knocked on the door and said a policeman wanted to talk to me and I had to open the door. And she said she wouldn't let him take me away and she promised. So I picked Toby up and opened the door.

And there was a policeman outside the door and he said, "Are you Christopher Boone?"

And I said I was.

And he said, "Your father says you've run away. Is that right?"

And I said, "Yes."

And he said, "Is this your mother?" and he pointed at Mother.

And I said, "Yes."

And he said, "Why did you run away?"

And I said, "Because Father killed Wellington, who is a dog, and I was frightened of him."

And he said, "So I've been told." And then he said, "Do you want to go back to Swindon to your father or do you want to stay here?"

And I said, "I want to stay here."

And he said, "And how do you feel about that?"

And I said, "I want to stay here."

And the policeman said, "Hang on. I'm asking your mother."

And Mother said, "He told Christopher I was dead."

And the policeman said, "OK, let's . . . let's not get into an argument about who said what here. I just want to know whether—"

And Mother said, "Of course he can stay."

And then the policeman said, "Well, I think that probably settles it as far as I'm concerned."

And I said, "Are you going to take me back to Swindon?"

And he said, "No."

And then I was happy because I could live with Mother.

And the policeman said, "If your husband turns up and causes any trouble, just give us a ring. Otherwise, you're going to have to sort this out between yourselves."

And then the policeman went away and I had my tomato soup and Mr. Shears stacked up some boxes in the spare room so he could put a blowup mattress on the floor for me to sleep on, and I went to sleep.

And then I woke up because there were people shouting in the flat and it was 2:31 a.m. And one of the people was Father and I was frightened. But there wasn't a lock on the door of the spare room.

And Father shouted, "I'm talking to her whether you like it or not. And I am not going to be told what to do by you of all people."

And Mother shouted, "Roger. Don't. Just——"

And Mr. Shears shouted, "I'm not being spoken to like that in my own home."

And Father shouted, "I'll talk to you how I damn well like."

And Mother shouted, "You have no right to be here."

And Father shouted, "No right? No right? He's my fucking son, in case you've forgotten."

And Mother shouted, "What in God's name did you think you were playing at, saying those things to him?"

And Father shouted, "What was I playing at? You were the one that bloody left."

And Mother shouted, "So you decided to just wipe me out of his life altogether?"

And Mr. Shears shouted, "Now let's us all just calm down here, shall we?"

And Father shouted, "Well, isn't that what you wanted?"

And Mother shouted, "I wrote to him every week. Every week."

And Father shouted, "Wrote to him? What the fuck use is writing to him?"

And Mr. Shears shouted, "Whoa, whoa, whoa."

And Father shouted, "I cooked his meals. I cleaned his clothes. I looked after him every weekend. I looked after him when he was ill. I took him to the doctor. I worried myself sick every time he wandered off somewhere at night. I went to school every time he got into a fight. And you? What? You wrote him some fucking letters."

And Mother shouted, "So you thought it was OK to tell him his mother was dead?"

And Mr. Shears shouted, "Now is not the time."

And Father shouted, "You, butt out or I'll—"

And Mother shouted, "Ed, for God's sake—"

And Father said, "I'm going to see him. And if you try to stop me—"

And then Father came into my room. But I was holding my Swiss Army knife with the saw blade out in case he grabbed me. And Mother came into the room as well, and she said, "It's OK, Christopher. I won't let him do anything. You're all right."

And Father bent down on his knees near the bed and he said, "Christopher?"

But I didn't say anything.

And he said, "Christopher, I'm really, really sorry. About everything. About Wellington. About the letters. About making you run away. I never meant . . . I promise I will never do anything like that again. Hey. Come on, kiddo."

And then he held up his right hand and spread his fingers out in a fan so that I could touch his fingers, but I didn't because I was frightened.

And Father said, "Shit. Christopher, please."

And there were tears dripping off his face.

And no one said anything for a while.

And then Mother said, "I think you should go now," but she was talking to Father, not me.

And then the policeman came back because Mr. Shears had rung the police station and he told Father to calm down and he took him out of the flat.

And Mother said, "You go back to sleep now. Everything is going to be all right. I promise."

And then I went back to sleep.

229. And when I was asleep I had one of my favorite dreams. Sometimes I have it during the day, but then it's a daydream. But I often have it at night as well.

And in the dream nearly everyone on the earth is dead, because they have caught a virus. But it's not like a normal virus. It's like a computer virus. And people catch it because of the meaning of something an infected person says and the meaning of what they do with their faces when they say it, which means that people can also get it from watching an infected person on television, which means that it spreads around the world really quickly.

And when people get the virus they just sit on the sofa and do nothing and they don't eat or drink and so they die. But sometimes I have different versions of the dream, like when you can see two versions of a film, the ordinary one and the *director's cut,* like **Blade Runner.** And in some versions of the dream the virus makes them crash their cars or walk into the sea and drown, or jump into rivers, and I think that this version is better because then there aren't bodies of dead people everywhere.

And eventually there is no one left in the world except people who don't look at other people's faces and who don't know what these pictures mean

and these people are all special people like me. And they like being on their own and I hardly ever see them because they are like okapi in the jungle in the Congo, which are a kind of antelope and very shy and rare.

And I can go anywhere in the world and I know that no one is going to talk to me or touch me or ask me a question. But if I don't want to go anywhere I don't have to, and I can stay at home and eat broccoli and oranges and licorice laces all the time, or I can play computer games for a whole week, or I can just sit in the corner of the room and rub a £1 coin back and forward over the ripple shapes on the surface of the radiator. And I wouldn't have to go to France.

And I go out of Father's house and I walk down the street, and it is very quiet even though it is the middle of the day and I can't hear any noise except birds singing and wind and sometimes buildings falling down in the distance, and if I stand very close to traffic lights I can hear a little click as the colors change.

And I go into other people's houses and play at being a detective and I can break the windows to get in because the people are dead and it doesn't matter. And I go into shops and take things I want, like pink biscuits or PJ's Raspberry and Mango Smoothie or computer games or books or videos.

And I take a ladder from Father's van and I climb up onto the roof, and when I get to the edge of the roof I put the ladder across the gap and I climb to the next roof, because in a dream you are allowed to do anything.

And then I find someone's car keys and I get into their car and I drive, and it doesn't matter if I bump into things and I drive to the sea, and I park the car and I get out and there is rain pouring down. And I take an ice cream from a shop and eat it. And then I walk down to the beach. And the beach is covered in sand and big rocks and there is a lighthouse on a point but the light is not on because the lighthouse keeper is dead.

And I stand in the surf and it comes up and over my shoes. And I don't go swimming in case there are sharks. And I stand and look at the horizon and I take out my long metal ruler and I hold it up against the line between the sea and the sky and I demonstrate that the line is a curve and the earth is round. And the way the surf comes up and over my shoes and then goes down again is in a rhythm, like music or drumming.

And then I get some dry clothes from the house of a family who are dead. And I go home to Father's house, except it's not Father's house anymore, it's mine. And I make myself some Gobi Aloo Sag with red food coloring in it and some strawberry milk shake for a drink, and then I watch a video about the solar system and I play some computer games and I go to bed.

And then the dream is finished and I am happy.

233. The next morning I had fried tomatoes for breakfast and a tin of green beans which Mother heated up in a saucepan.

In the middle of breakfast, Mr. Shears said, "OK. He can stay for a few days."

And Mother said, "He can stay as long as he needs to stay."

And Mr. Shears said, "This flat is hardly big enough for two people, let alone three."

And Mother said, "He can understand what you're saying, you know."

And Mr. Shears said, "What's he going to do? There's no school for him to go to. We've both got jobs. It's bloody ridiculous."

And Mother said, "Roger. That's enough."

Then she made me some Red Zinger herbal tea with sugar in it but I didn't like it, and she said, "You can stay for as long as you want to stay."

And after Mr. Shears had gone to work she made a telephone call to the office and took what is called *Compassionate Leave*, which is when someone in your family dies or is ill.

Then she said we had to go and buy some clothes for me to wear and some pajamas and a toothbrush and a flannel. So we went out of the flat and we walked to the main road, which was Hill Lane, which was the A4088, and it was really crowded and we caught a number 266 bus to Brent Cross Shopping Centre. Except there were too many people in John Lewis and I was frightened and I lay down on the floor next to the wristwatches and I screamed and Mother had to take me home in a taxi.

Then she had to go back to the shopping center to buy me some clothes and some pajamas and a toothbrush and a flannel, so I stayed in the spare room while she was gone because I didn't want to be in the same room as Mr. Shears because I was frightened of him.

And when Mother got home she brought me a glass of strawberry milk shake and showed me my new pajamas, and the pattern on them was 5-pointed blue stars on a purple background like this

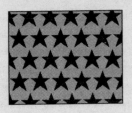

And I said, "I have to go back to Swindon."

And Mother said, "Christopher, you've only just got here."

And I said, "I have to go back because I have to sit my maths A level."

And Mother said, "You're doing maths A level?"

And I said, "Yes. I'm taking it on Wednesday and Thursday and Friday next week."

And Mother said, "God."

And I said, "The Reverend Peters is going to be the invigilator."

And Mother said, "I mean, that's really good."

And I said, "I'm going to get an A grade. And that's why I have to go back to Swindon. Except I don't want to see Father. So I have to go to Swindon with you."

Then Mother put her hands over her face and breathed out hard, and she said, "I don't know whether that's going to be possible."

And I said, "But I have to go."

And Mother said, "Let's talk about this some other time, OK?"

And I said, "OK. But I have to go to Swindon."

And she said, "Christopher, please."

And I drank some of my milk shake.

And later on, at 10:31 p.m. I went out onto the balcony to find out whether I could see any stars, but there weren't any because of all the clouds and what is called *light pollution*, which is light from streetlights and car headlights and floodlights and lights in buildings reflecting off tiny particles in the atmosphere and getting in the way of light from the stars. So I went back inside.

But I couldn't sleep. And I got out of bed at 2:07 a.m. and I felt scared of Mr. Shears so I went downstairs and out of the front door into Chapter Road. And there was no one in the street and it was quieter than it was during the day, even though you could hear traffic in the distance and sirens, so it made me feel calmer. And I walked down Chapter Road and looked at all the cars and the patterns the phone wires made against the orange clouds and the things that people had in their front gardens, like a gnome and a cooker and a tiny pond and a teddy bear.

Then I heard two people coming along the road, so I crouched down between the end of a skip and a Ford Transit van, and they were talking in a language that wasn't English, but they didn't see me. And there were two tiny brass cogs in the dirty water in the gutter by my feet, like cogs from a windup watch.

And I liked it between the skip and the Ford Transit van so I stayed there for a long time. And I looked out at the street. And the only colors you could see were orange and black and mixtures of orange and black. And you couldn't tell what colors the cars would be during the day.

And I wondered whether you could tessellate crosses, and I worked out that you could by imagining this picture in my head

And then I heard Mother's voice and she was shouting, "Christopher . . . ? Christopher . . . ?" and she was running down the road, so I came out from between the skip and the Ford Transit van and she ran up to me and said, "Jesus Christ," and she stood in front of me and pointed her finger at my face and said, "If you ever do that again, I swear to God, Christopher, I love you, but . . . I don't know what I'll do."

So she made me promise never to leave the flat on my own because it was dangerous and because you couldn't trust people in London because they were strangers. And the next day she had to go to the shops again and she made me promise not to answer the door if anyone rang the bell. And when she came back she brought some food pellets for Toby and three *Star Trek* videos and I watched them in the living room until Mr. Shears came home and then I went into the spare room again. And I wished that 451c Chapter Road, London NW2 5NG, had a garden but it didn't.

And the day after that the office where Mother worked rang and told her she couldn't come back to work because they had got someone else to do her job for her, and she was really angry and she said that it was illegal and she was going to complain, but Mr. Shears said, "Don't be a bloody fool. It was a temporary job, for Christ's sake."

And when Mother came into the spare room before I went to sleep I said, "I have to go to Swindon to take my A level."

And she said, "Christopher, not now. I'm getting phone calls from your father threatening to take me to court. I'm getting it in the neck from Roger. It's not a good time."

And I said, "But I have to go because it's been arranged and the Reverend Peters is going to invigilate."

And she said, "Look. It's only an exam. I can ring the school. We can get it postponed. You can take it some other time."

And I said, "I can't take it another time. It's been arranged. And I've done lots of revision. And Mrs. Gascoyne said we could use a room at school."

And Mother said, "Christopher, I am just about holding this together. But I am this close to losing it, all right? So just give me some—"

Then she stopped talking and she put her hand over her mouth and she stood up and went out of the room. And I started feeling a pain in my chest like I did on the underground because I thought I wasn't going to be able to go back to Swindon and take my A level.

And the next morning I looked out of the window in the dining room to count the cars in the street to see whether it was going to be a **Quite Good Day** or a **Good Day** or a **Super Good Day** or a **Black Day,** but it wasn't like being on the bus to school because you could look out of the window for as long as you wanted and see as many cars as you wanted, and I looked out of the window for three hours and I saw 5 red cars in a row and 4 yellow cars in a row, which meant it was both a **Good Day** and a **Black Day,** so the system didn't work anymore. But if I concentrated on counting the cars it stopped me from thinking about my A level and the pain in my chest.

And in the afternoon Mother took me to Hampstead Heath in a taxi and we sat on the top of a hill and looked at the planes coming into Heathrow Airport in the distance. And I had a red ice lolly from an ice cream van. And Mother said she had rung Mrs. Gascoyne and told her that I was going to take my maths A level next year, so I threw my red ice lolly away and I screamed for a long time and the pain in my chest hurt so much that it was hard to breathe and a man came up and asked if I was OK and Mother said, "Well, what does it look like to you?" and he went away.

And then I was tired from screaming and Mother took me back to the flat in another taxi and the next morning was Saturday and she told Mr. Shears to go out and get me some books about science and maths from the library, and they were called *100 Number Puzzles* and *The Origins of the Universe* and *Nuclear Power,* but they were for children and they were not very good so I didn't read them, and Mr. Shears said, "Well, it's nice to know my contribution is appreciated."

And I hadn't eaten anything since I threw away the red ice lolly on Hampstead Heath, so Mother made me a chart with stars on it like when I was very small and she filled a measuring jug with Complan and strawberry flavoring and I got a bronze star for drinking 200 ml and a silver star for drinking 400 ml and a gold star for drinking 600 ml.

And when Mother and Mr. Shears argued I took the little radio from the kitchen and I went and sat in the spare room and I tuned it halfway between two stations so that all I could hear was white noise and I turned the volume up really loud and I held it against my ear and the sound filled my head and it hurt so that I couldn't feel any other sort of hurt, like the hurt in my chest, and I couldn't hear Mother and Mr. Shears arguing and I couldn't think about not doing my A level or the fact that there wasn't a garden at 451c Chapter Road, London NW2 5NG, or the fact that I couldn't see the stars.

And then it was Monday. And it was very late at night and Mr. Shears came into my room and woke me up and he had been drinking beer because he smelled like Father did when he had been drinking beer with Rhodri. And he said, "You think you're so fucking clever, don't you. Don't you ever, ever think about other people for one second, eh? Well, I bet you're really pleased with yourself now, aren't you."

And then Mother came in and pulled him out of the room and said, "Christopher, I'm sorry. I'm really, really sorry."

The next morning, after Mr. Shears had gone to work, Mother packed lots of her clothes into two suitcases and told me to come downstairs and bring Toby and get into the car. And she put the suitcases into the boot and we drove off. But it was Mr. Shears's car and I said, "Are you stealing the car?"

And she said, "I'm just borrowing it."

And I said, "Where are we going?"

And she said, "We're going home."

And I said, "Do you mean home in Swindon?"

And she said, "Yes."

And I said, "Is Father going to be there?"

And she said, "Please, Christopher. Don't give me any hassle right now, OK?"

And I said, "I don't want to be with Father."

And she said, "Just . . . Just . . . It's going to be all right, Christopher, OK? It's going to be all right."

And I said, "Are we going back to Swindon so I can do my maths A level?"

And Mother said, "What?"

And I said, "I'm meant to be doing my maths A level to-morrow."

And Mother spoke very slowly and she said, "We are going back to Swindon because if we stay in London any longer . . . someone was going to get hurt. And I don't necessarily mean you."

And I said, "What do you mean?"

And she said, "Now I need you to be quiet for a while."

And I said, "How long do you want me to be quiet for?"

And she said, "Jesus." And then she said, "Half an hour, Christopher. I need you to be quiet for half an hour."

And we drove all the way to Swindon and it took 3 hours 12 minutes and we had to stop for petrol and Mother bought me a Milkybar but I didn't eat it. And we got caught in a long traffic jam which was caused by people slowing down to look at an accident on the other carriageway. And I tried to work out a formula to determine whether a traffic jam would be caused just by people slowing down and how this was influenced by (a) the density of traffic, and (b) the speed of the traffic, and (c) how quickly drivers braked when they saw the brake of the lights of the car in front coming on. But I was too tired because I hadn't slept the night before because I was thinking about not being able to do my maths A level. So I fell asleep.

And when we got to Swindon Mother had keys to the house and we went in and she said, "Hello?" but there was no one there because it was 1:23 p.m. And I was frightened but Mother said I would be safe, so I went up to my room and closed the door. I took Toby out of my pocket and I let him run around and I played **Minesweeper** and I did the Expert Version in 174 seconds, which was 75 seconds longer than my best time.

And then it was 6:35 p.m. and I heard Father come home

in his van and I moved the bed up against the door so he couldn't get in and he came into the house and he and Mother shouted at each other.

And Father shouted, "How the fuck did you get in here?"

And Mother shouted, "This is my house, too, in case you've forgotten."

And Father shouted, "Is your fucking fancy man here as well?"

And then I picked up the bongo drums that Uncle Terry had bought me and I knelt down in the corner of the room and I pressed my head into the join between the two walls and I banged the drums and I groaned and I carried on doing this for an hour and then Mother came into the room and said Father had gone. And she said Father had gone to stay with Rhodri for a while and we would get a place to live of our own in the next few weeks.

Then I went into the garden and I found Toby's cage behind the shed and I brought it inside and I cleaned it and put Toby back in it.

And I asked Mother if I could do my maths A level the next day.

And she said, "I'm sorry, Christopher."

And I said, "Can I do my maths A level?"

And she said, "You're not listening to me, are you, Christopher."

And I said, "I'm listening to you."

And Mother said, "I told you. I rang your headmistress. I told her you were in London. I told her you'd do it next year."

And I said, "But I'm here now and I can take it."

And Mother said, "I'm sorry, Christopher. I was trying to do things properly. I was trying not to mess things up."

And my chest began hurting again and I folded my arms and I rocked backward and forward and groaned.

And Mother said, "I didn't know we'd be coming back."

But I carried on groaning and rocking backward and forward.

And Mother said, "Come on. This isn't going to solve anything."

Then she asked if I wanted to watch one of my **Blue Planet** videos, about life under the Arctic ice or the migration of humpback whales, but I didn't say anything because I knew I wasn't going to be able to do my maths A level and it was like pressing your thumbnail against a radiator when it's really hot and the pain starts and it makes you want to cry and the pain keeps hurting even when you take your thumb away from the radiator.

Then Mother made me some carrots and broccoli and ketchup, but I didn't eat them.

And I didn't sleep that night either.

The next day Mother drove me to school in Mr. Shears's car because we missed the bus. And when we were getting into the car, Mrs. Shears came across the road and said to Mother, "You've got a fucking nerve."

And Mother said, "Get into the car, Christopher."

But I couldn't get into the car because the door was locked.

And Mrs. Shears said, "So, has he finally dumped you, too?"

Then Mother opened her door and got into the car and unlocked my door and I got in and we drove away.

And when we got to school Siobhan said, "So you're Christopher's mother." And Siobhan said that she was glad to see me again and she asked if I was OK and I said I was tired. And Mother explained that I was upset because I couldn't do my maths A level so I hadn't been eating properly or sleeping properly.

And then Mother went away and I drew a picture of a bus using perspective so that I didn't think about the pain in my chest and it looked like this

And after lunch Siobhan said that she had spoken to Mrs. Gascoyne and she still had my A-level papers in 3 sealed envelopes in her desk.

So I asked if I could still do my A level.

And Siobhan said, "I think so. We're going to ring the Reverend Peters this afternoon to make sure he can still come in and be your invigilator. And Mrs. Gascoyne is going to write a letter to the examination board to say that you're going to take the exam after all. And hopefully they'll say that that's OK. But we can't know that for sure." Then she stopped talking for a few seconds. "I thought I should tell you now. So you could think about it."

And I said, "So I could think about what?"

And she said, "Is this what you want to do, Christopher?"

And I thought about the question and I wasn't sure what the answer was because I wanted to do my maths A level but I was very tired and when I tried to think about maths my brain didn't work properly and when I tried to remember certain facts, like the logarithmic formula for the approximate number of prime numbers not greater than **x,** I couldn't remember them and this made me frightened.

And Siobhan said, "You don't have to do it, Christopher. If you say you don't want to do it no one is going to be angry with you. And it won't be wrong or illegal or stupid. It will just be what you want and that will be fine."

And I said, "I want to do it," because I don't like it when I put things in my timetable and I have to take them out again, because when I do that it makes me feel sick.

And Siobhan said, "OK."

And she rang the Reverend Peters and he came into school at 3:27 p.m. and he said, "So, young man, are we ready to roll?"

And I did **Paper 1** of my maths A level sitting in the Art Room. And the Reverend Peters was the invigilator and he sat at a desk while I did the exam and he read a book called *The Cost of Discipleship* by Dietrich Bonhoeffer and ate a sandwich. And in the middle of the exam he went and smoked a cigarette outside the window, but he watched me through the window in case I cheated.

And when I opened the paper and read through it I couldn't think how to answer any of the questions and also I couldn't breathe properly. And I wanted to hit somebody or stab them with my Swiss Army knife, but there wasn't anyone to hit or stab with my Swiss Army knife except the Reverend Peters and he was very tall and if I hit him or stabbed him with my Swiss Army knife he wouldn't be my invigilator for the rest of the exam. So I took deep breaths like Siobhan said I should do when

I want to hit someone in school and I counted 50 breaths and did cubes of the cardinal numbers as I counted, like this

1, 8, 27, 64, 125, 216, 343, 512, 729, 1000, 1331, 1728, 2197, 2744, 3375, 4096, 4913 ... etc.

And that made me feel a little calmer. But the exam was 2 hours long and 20 minutes had already gone so I had to work really fast and I didn't have time to check my answers properly.

And that night, just after I got home, Father came back to the house and I screamed but Mother said she wouldn't let anything bad happen to me and I went into the garden and lay down and looked at the stars in the sky and made myself negligible. And when Father came out of the house he looked at me for a long time and then he punched the fence and made a hole in it and went away.

And I slept a little bit that night because I was doing my maths A level. And I had some spinach soup for supper.

And the next day I did **Paper 2** and the Reverend Peters read *The Cost of Discipleship* by Dietrich Bonhoeffer, but this time he didn't smoke a cigarette and Siobhan made me go into the toilets before the exam and sit on my own and do breathing and counting.

And I was playing **The 11th Hour** on my computer that evening when a taxi stopped outside the house. Mr. Shears was in the taxi and he got out of the taxi and threw a big cardboard box of things belonging to Mother onto the lawn. And they were a hair dryer and some knickers and some L'Oréal shampoo and a box of muesli and two books, *DIANA: Her True Story* by Andrew Morton and *Rivals* by Jilly Cooper, and a photograph of me in a silver frame. And the glass in the photograph frame broke when it fell onto the grass.

Then he got some keys out of his pocket and got into his car and drove away and Mother ran out of the house and she ran into the street and shouted, "Don't fucking bother coming back, either!" And she threw the box of muesli and it hit the boot of his car as he drove away and Mrs. Shears was looking out of her window when Mother did this.

The next day I did **Paper 3** and the Reverend Peters read the *Daily Mail* and smoked three cigarettes.

And this was my favorite question

Prove the following result:

A triangle with sides that can be written in the form $n^2 + 1$, $n^2 - 1$ and $2n$ (where $n > 1$) is right-angled.

Show, by means of a counterexample, that the converse is false.

And I was going to write out how I answered the question except Siobhan said it wasn't very interesting, but I said it was. And she said people wouldn't want to read the answers to a maths question in a book, and she said I could put the answer in an *Appendix*, which is an extra chapter at the end of a book which people can read if they want to. And that is what I have done.

And then my chest didn't hurt so much and it was easier to breathe. But I still felt sick because I didn't know if I'd done well in the exam and because I didn't know if the examination board would allow my exam paper to be considered after Mrs. Gascoyne had told them I wasn't going to take it.

And it's best if you know a good thing is going to happen, like an eclipse or getting a microscope for Christmas. And it's bad if you know a bad thing is going to happen, like having a filling or going to France. But I think it is worst if you don't know whether it is a good thing or a bad thing which is going to happen.

And Father came round to the house that night and I was sitting on the sofa watching *University Challenge* and just answering the science questions. And he stood in the doorway of the living room and he said, "Don't scream, OK, Christopher. I'm not going to hurt you."

And Mother was standing behind him so I didn't scream.

Then he came a bit closer to me and he crouched down like you do with dogs to show that you are not an Aggressor and he said, "I wanted to ask you how the exam went."

But I didn't say anything.

And Mother said, "Tell him, Christopher."

But I still didn't say anything.

And Mother said, "Please, Christopher."

So I said, "I don't know if I got all the questions right because I was really tired and I hadn't eaten any food so I couldn't think properly."

And then Father nodded and he didn't say anything for a short while. Then he said "Thank you."

And I said, "What for?"

And he said, "Just . . . thank you." Then he said, "I'm very proud of you, Christopher. Very proud. I'm sure you did really well."

And then he went away and I watched the rest of *University Challenge.*

And the next week Father told Mother she had to move out

of the house, but she couldn't because she didn't have any money to pay rent for a flat. And I asked if Father would be arrested and go to prison for killing Wellington because we could live in the house if he was in prison. But Mother said the police would only arrest Father if Mrs. Shears did what is called *pressing charges*, which is telling the police you want them to arrest someone for a crime, because the police don't arrest people for little crimes unless you ask them and Mother said that killing a dog was only a little crime.

But then everything was OK because Mother got a job on the till in a garden center and the doctor gave her pills to take every morning to stop her from feeling sad, except that sometimes they made her dizzy and she fell over if she stood up too fast. So we moved into a room in a big house that was made of red bricks. And the bed was in the same room as the kitchen and I didn't like it because it was small and the corridor was painted brown and there was a toilet and a bathroom that other people used and Mother had to clean it before I used it or I wouldn't use it and sometimes I wet myself because other people were in the bathroom. And the corridor outside the room smelled like gravy and the bleach they use to clean the toilets at school. And inside the room it smelled like socks and pine air freshener.

And I didn't like waiting to find out about my maths A level. And whenever I thought about the future I couldn't see anything clearly in my head and that made a panic start. So Siobhan said I shouldn't think about the future. She said, "Just think about today. Think about things that have happened. Especially about good things that have happened."

And one of the good things was that Mother bought me a wooden puzzle which looked like this

And you had to detach the top part of the puzzle from the bottom part, and it was really difficult.

And another good thing was that I helped Mother paint her room *White with a Hint of Wheat,* except I got paint in my hair and she wanted to wash it out by rubbing shampoo on my head when I was in the bath, but I wouldn't let her, so there was paint in my hair for 5 days and then I cut it out with a pair of scissors.

But there were more bad things than good things.

And one of them was that Mother didn't get back from work till 5:30 p.m. so I had to go to Father's house between 3:49 p.m. and 5:30 p.m., because I wasn't allowed to be on my own and Mother said I didn't have a choice, so I pushed the bed against the door in case Father tried to come in. And sometimes he tried to talk to me through the door, but I didn't answer him. And sometimes I heard him sitting on the floor outside the door quietly for a long time.

And another bad thing was that Toby died because he was 2 years and 7 months old, which is very old for a rat, and I said I wanted to bury him, but Mother didn't have a garden, so I buried him in a big plastic pot of earth like a pot you put a plant in. And I said I wanted another rat but Mother said I couldn't have one because the room was too small.

And I solved the puzzle because I worked out that there

were two bolts inside the puzzle and they were tunnels with metal rods in them like this

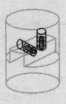

And you had to hold the puzzle so that both rods slid to the end of their tunnels and they weren't crossing the intersection between the two pieces of the puzzle and then you could pull them apart.

And Mother picked me up from Father's house one day after she had finished work and Father said, "Christopher, can I have a talk with you?"

And I said, "No."

And Mother said, "It's OK. I'll be here."

And I said, "I don't want to talk to Father."

And Father said, "I'll do you a deal." And he was holding the kitchen timer, which is a big plastic tomato sliced through the middle, and he twisted it and it started ticking. And he said, "Five minutes, OK? That's all. Then you can go."

So I sat on the sofa and he sat on the armchair and Mother was in the hallway and Father said, "Christopher, look . . . Things can't go on like this. I don't know about you, but this . . . this just hurts too much. You being in the house but refusing to talk to me . . . You have to learn to trust me . . . And I don't care how long it takes . . . If it's a minute one day and two minutes the next and three minutes the next and it takes years I don't care. Because this is important. This is more important than anything else."

And then he tore a little strip of skin away from the side of the thumbnail on his left hand.

And then he said, "Let's call it . . . let's call it a project. A project we have to do together. You have to spend more time with me. And I . . . I have to show you that you can trust me. And it will be difficult at first because . . . because it's a difficult project. But it will get better. I promise."

Then he rubbed the sides of his forehead with his fingertips, and he said, "You don't have to say anything, not right now. You just have to think about it. And, um . . . I've got you a present. To show you that I really mean what I say. And to say sorry. And because . . . well, you'll see what I mean."

Then he got out of the armchair and he walked over to the kitchen door and opened it and there was a big cardboard box on the floor and there was a blanket in it and he bent down and put his hands inside the box and he took a little sandy-colored dog out.

Then he came back through and gave me the dog. And he said, "He's two months old. And he's a golden retriever."

And the dog sat in my lap and I stroked it.

And no one said anything for a while.

Then Father said, "Christopher, I would never, ever do anything to hurt you."

Then no one said anything.

Then Mother came into the room and said, "You won't be able to take him away with you, I'm afraid. The bed-sit's too small. But your father's going to look after him here. And you can come and take him out for walks whenever you want."

And I said, "Does he have a name?"

And Father said, "No. You can decide what to call him."

And the dog chewed my finger.

And then it was 5 minutes and the tomato alarm went. So Mother and I drove back to her room.

And the next week there was a lightning storm and the lightning hit a big tree in the park near Father's house and knocked it down and men came and cut the branches up with chain saws and carried the logs away on a lorry, and all that was left was a big black pointed stump made of carbonized wood.

And I got the results of my maths A level and I got an A grade, which is the best result, and it made me feel like this

And I called the dog Sandy. And Father bought him a collar and a lead and I was allowed to take him for walks to the shop and back. And I played with him with a rubber bone.

And Mother got flu and I had to spend three days with Father and stay in his house. But it was OK because Sandy slept on my bed so he would bark if anyone came into the room during the night. And Father made a vegetable patch in the garden and I helped him. And we planted carrots and peas and spinach and I'm going to pick them and eat them when they're ready.

And I went to a bookshop with Mother and I bought a book called *Further Maths for A Level* and Father told Mrs. Gascoyne that I was going to take A-level further maths next year and she said "OK."

And I am going to pass it and get an A grade. And in two years' time I am going to take A-level physics and get an A grade.

And then, when I've done that, I am going to go to university in another town. And it doesn't have to be in London because don't like London and there are universities in lots of places and not all of them are in big cities. And I can live in a flat with a garden and a proper toilet. And I can take Sandy and my books and my computer.

And then I will get a First Class Honors degree and I will become a scientist.

And I know I can do this because I went to London on my own, and because I solved the mystery of **Who Killed Wellington?** and I found my mother and I was brave and I wrote a book and that means I can do anything.

APPENDIX

Prove the following result:

A triangle with sides that can be written in the form $n^2 + 1$, $n^2 - 1$ and $2n$ (where $n > 1$) is right-angled.

Show, by means of a counterexample, that the converse is false.

ANSWER

First we must determine which is the longest side of a triangle with sides that can be written in the form $n^2 + 1$, $n^2 - 1$ and $2n$ (where $n > 1$)

$$n^2 + 1 - 2n = (n - 1)^2$$

and if $n > 1$ then $(n - 1)^2 > 0$

therefore $n^2 + 1 - 2n > 0$

therefore $n^2 + 1 > 2n$

Similarly $(n^2 + 1) - (n^2 - 1) = 2$

therefore $n^2 + 1 > n^2 - 1$

This means that $n^2 + 1$ is the longest side of a triangle with sides that can be written in the form $n^2 + 1$, $n^2 - 1$ and $2n$ (where $n > 1$).

This can also be shown by means of the following graph (but this doesn't prove anything):

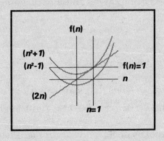

According to Pythagoras's theorem, if the sum of the squares of the two shorter sides equals the square of the hypotenuse, then the triangle is right-angled. Therefore to prove that the triangle is right-angled we need to show that this is the case.

The sum of the squares of the shorter two sides is $(n^2 - 1)^2 + (2n)^2$

$$(n^2 - 1)^2 + (2n)^2 = n^4 - 2n^2 + 1 + 4n^2 = \underline{n^4 + 2n^2 + 1}$$

The square of the hypotenuse is $(n^2 + 1)^2$

$$(n^2 + 1)^2 = \underline{n^4 + 2n^2 + 1}$$

Therefore the sum of the squares of the shorter two sides is equal to the square of the hypotenuse and the triangle is right-angled.

And the converse of "A triangle with sides that can be written in the form $n^2 + 1$, $n^2 - 1$ and $2n$ (where $n > 1$) is right-angled" is "A triangle that is right-angled has sides whose lengths can be written in the form $n^2 + 1$, $n^2 - 1$ and $2n$ (where $n > 1$)."

And a counterexample means finding a triangle which is right-angled but whose sides cannot be written in the form $n^2 + 1$, $n^2 - 1$ and $2n$ (where $n > 1$).

So let the hypotenuse of the right-angled triangle **ABC** be **AB**.

and let **AB** = 65

and let **BC** = 60

Then $CA = \sqrt{(AB^2 - BC^2)}$
$$= \sqrt{(65^2 - 60^2)} = \sqrt{(4225 - 3600)} = \sqrt{625} = 25$$

Let $AB = n^2 + 1 = 65$

then $n = \sqrt{(65 - 1)} = \sqrt{64} = 8$

therefore $(n^2 - 1) = 64 - 1 = 63 \neq BC = 60 \neq CA = 25$

and $2n = 16 \neq BC = 60 \neq CA = 25$

Therefore the triangle **ABC** is right-angled but it does not have sides which can be written in the form $n^2 + 1$, $n^2 - 1$ and $2n$ (where $n > 1$). QED